THE MONK

AND OTHER STORIES

HL SERRA

Other books by HL Serra:

NILO Ha Tien —A Novel of Naval Intelligence in Cambodia (2009)

OOPS! A War Story for Children (2009)

The Sihanoukville Inquiry —A Play in Two Acts (2009)

The Monk
and
Other Stories

HL Serra

authorHOUSE®

AuthorHouse™
1663 Liberty Drive
Bloomington, IN 47403
www.authorhouse.com
Phone: 1-800-839-8640

Published by AuthorHouse   06/15/2012

ISBN: 978-1-4772-2018-4 (sc)
ISBN: 978-1-4772-2017-7 (e)

Library of Congress Control Number: 2012910670

Detail from ironwork railings at 1, rue Réamur, Paris 12/07 © HL Serra

ACKNOWLEDGEMENTS

I want to thank John Nelson Ferrara, former LT USN, without whom the "Pirate Islands" story would not have been possible. The facts and details come from a mission I had planned but was unable to perform at the end of my NILO tour in Ha Tien. John picked up the ball and ran with it. Knowing he executed the mission completes my NILO tour. I was particularly taken by John's description of "the jungle's night song."

Crane Davis, former CAPT USMC, once again provided all the cover art, logos and maps for this volume of short stories and vignettes, and plenty of support with his wry good humor, for all of which I thank him.

Ralph Christopher, fellow River Rat (and author of a book of that name), once again provided encouragement to publish this volume, and provided important tactical details.

JR Reddig, naval intelligence CAPT USN (ret.), provided excellent advice from the balcony which helped me decide which stories to include.

I thank Chris Serra for his editorial overview and subtle persuasive powers in encouraging me to drop some and add some.

HL Serra
San Diego CA
June 13, 2012

Contents

The War...

Before...

And After...

The War...

I. Ha Tien and Saigon
1969-70

MASS, SAIGON

Medici crossed the grassy patch between the old winery that housed naval staff and Admiral Zumwalt's residence. The open porch smelled of burning incense and groaned under the weight of thirty navy men concentrating on the words of Father Commander Bright.

"Oh, Lord, we beseech Thee to defend us in our pitched battle with the evil forces of communism in this bleeding, beleaguered nation, striving so gallantly to preserve its independence as we once did against the forces of oppression. Lord, let us prevail and rend asunder the serpent from the north that seeks to dominate this nation and resist our efforts to bring democracy to the hearts and minds of the Veetneese." He bowed his head to his chest until it rested on a puffy, florid chin. A few in the congregation served "Amens" toward the priest like volleyballs.

Bright raised his head. "And now the Sunday mass announcements will be read by Captain Rannette."

A thin pale man stepped in front of the priest and read from a white card in his hand.

"The second collection today will be for the benefit of Admiral Zumwalt's Pigs and Chickens Fund."

He smiled and nodded toward the Admiral who restrained a smile and nodded his head slightly.

"As you know, the Admiral's fund seeks to supplement the diet of our Veetneese Navy counterparts with protein, which the average Asian's diet lacks. We buy piglets and baby chicks and supply them to each Veetneese navy base. As the flocks grow the Veetneese diet will be modified to include a greater daily ration of chicken or pork which will increase the energy and stamina of our counterparts, so they can perform more demanding physical labor and undertake more frequent combat patrols, twin goals of our Veetnamization program."

Rannette smiled modestly and looked back to the note card. Medici smirked. In his mind he pictured the photocopy cartoon passed around the staff offices: a large pig with a dominating sneer mounted for intercourse a hapless chicken whose eyes bulged like tennis balls. The caption read "Admiral's Pigs and Chickens Fund."

"There will be a memorial mass on Tuesday at 5 P.M. for LT(jg) Boggs of River Division 539 who was tragically killed last week while on ambush on the Vinh Te Canal at the Cambodian border," Rannette continued. "Anyone wishing to have his personal note of condolence included in the package of personal effects and Bronze Star award being sent to Boggs' family should turn it in to the casualty assistance control officer's clerk before noon Tuesday."

Rannette cleared his throat. Incense smoke, frankincense Medici guessed, filled the tiny porch. Others coughed and snorted.

"Finally, there will be a joint dinner of our congregation and the Veetneese-American Association on Thursday evening at 7 P.M. at their building across the street from the Le Qui Don Hotel." Rannette looked up. "You'll remember, gents, that the association includes a great number of widows of Vietnamese naval officers. It's our duty to be gracious to them."

Medici noticed several officers in the group blush deep red. They had been regularly "gracious" to some of the widows already, he thought.

Father Bright began the Introit but Medici could take no more. He stepped quietly down the stairs, convinced he had to get off headquarters staff as quickly as possible and get a field post.

Saigon 1969

THE MONK

Medici stirred, lifted his head and snorted the dampness from his sinuses. His right arm was asleep where his head lay on it. He clutched and unclutched his numb fingers to regain sensation. Sounds crept into his feeble consciousness. He heard FLAP-FLAP-FLAPping from the back of the room.

He raised his head and opened one eye. It was pitch dark except for the reflected white glare of the blank movie screen at the far end of the porch. The movie reel had run out long ago, and a strip of leader flogged the projector with each rotation.

He scanned the porch with his open eye. His pulse quickened. He saw the aftermath of an ambush. Navy river sailors lay strewn about the floor and akimbo on wooden chairs made from ammo crates. Belden, the army electrician in charge of the movie projector, lay with his head thrown back at a grotesque angle. The enormous space left by his missing front teeth aimed prominently at Medici. 'Have I slept through an attack?' Medici thought.

Then Belden snorted and gulped, others moved, and Medici realized this was the aftermath of the river sailors' celebration of another week surviving river ambushes on the Cambodian border.

Medici grunted when someone behind hit him on the head with a full beer can. He turned with a snap, expecting to see the bartender, but startled when he saw the assailant— the Monk, Advisory Team 55 Ha Tien's pet monkey— sitting on the bar.

The Monk tilted its head sideways and stared earnestly at Medici. Medici tilted his head the same way and returned the expression. He made the Monk blink. Medici rubbed the lump on his head, said, "Piss off, Monk," then laughed. The Monk turned away and picked up a can of Hamm's and took a sip. It shook its head spasmodically then grimaced and bared its teeth. Medici rested his head on his hand and thought, My new drinking partner— a lesser primate! Then he laughed, and reached over to pet the Monk, but it jumped back along the bar and spit in Medici's face, then filled its mouth with beer and spit again, dousing him. In a rage the Monk pounded its little fists on the bar between its crouched legs and jumped up and down like an ape, baring its teeth, hissing and hooting. Medici drew back from the bar, and the noise woke the others on the porch.

"Jeez, NILO, what'd you do to the Monk— pull his pud!" called Roberto Rubio, 'the Rube,' nominal owner of the Monk.

"He hit me with a beer can! And spit at me, then went bonkers," said Medici, his voice pitched with anger. "All I tried to do was pet him."

"NILO, you know he doesn't like to be touched without invitation. He's very territorial and possessive. Give him a break," the Rube said.

"He's got too damn much temper for me," said Medici. The Rube picked up the Monk like a baby. It clung to his neck, calming slowly, but glared at Medici as the Rube carried it out of the porch to its platform under the eaves of the junk sailors' hooch. Medici finished his beer, washed his face of the monkey's spittle, and went to bed mad.

Medici and the Monk steered each other a wide berth for the next week. The wide steering was more on Medici's part, since the Monk lived tethered to a ten-foot chain bolted securely to a heavy wooden workbench. That radius was the Monk's territory, and none dared invade it once the Monk's reputation for anger spread around the hill and riverboat base. Medici and the Monk eyed each other icily whenever Medici crossed the yard, neither forgetting a grudge easily. Once, Medici stopped halfway across the yard and made a quick lunge toward the Monk, sending it into alarums which quickly gave rise to action when the Monk heaved its feces at Medici with uncanny accuracy. Medici fumed.

The soldiers and sailors of the advisory team could not believe the intensity of the grudge between Medici and the monkey. Privately they concluded Medici, their Naval Intelligence Liaison

4

Officer, had been spending too much time by himself in Cambodia on spy missions, or needed to get laid, or both. Several days later, it came as a surprise to those who saw the event when Medici brought an enormous stalk of plump Cambodian bananas to the compound in the back of his jeep. They were for the Monk he said, a gesture of a new era of good feelings between man and his forbears. Medici wired the stalk to a hole in the rafter above the Monk's bench when the Rube took it for its after-dinner walk. Everyone wondered.

"NILO, you didn't poison those bananas?" the Rube asked. Medici, whom Rubio trusted, shook his head. They all waited and watched, but the Monk didn't die from poisoning. Rather, it flourished with a continuous source of fruit in addition to its diet of scraps from the Junkies' rations.

The Monk became protective and territorial about the stalk as the bananas dwindled. The Monk hissed at the Rube one afternoon when he tried to lower the stalk where it hung to bring the remaining bananas closer. Very possessive, Medici thought, just as the Rube had said.

When the stalk was down to the last ten bananas, the Monk grew positively jealous of anyone who tried to touch the bunch. It began to annoy the men on the hill, who had been eating only C-RATs on the river. The Monk was losing popularity points, and Medici knew it was time to strike.

From stalking the Monk for days, Medici knew it napped in the afternoon. One afternoon as the Monk slept and the junk sailors drifted about the yard, Medici eased his way to the corner of the Junkies' cabin to a spot where he could reach the stalk which held the last three bananas. The Monk slept fitfully a few feet away.

Medici breathed deep and gathered himself, Zen-like, for the attack. In one smooth, swift movement he slid around the corner, tore the three bananas from the stalk and sprinted out into the yard, eyes fixed on a stone where he turned and faced the Monk. Medici peeled and ate the first banana, then heaved its skin toward the bench where it bounced off the wall and landed on the Monk, awakening it with a start. Medici bared his teeth, hooted and hissed at the Monk, then pounded his fists on the dirt and jumped up and down. As a final taunt he waved the last two bananas in a wide arc.

The Monk hooted and hissed back. It saw Medici wave the last bananas, then glanced at the bare stalk and bounded from the workbench toward Medici, teeth bared, arms flailing.

Medici stood with his arms folded, smiling calmly as the Monk flew toward him. The junk sailors in the yard froze waiting to see the attack, wondering why Medici stood his ground rather than flee.

Then suddenly, mid-bound, the Monk reached the end of its ten-foot, four-and-three-quarter-inch chain, precisely where Medici— standing at eleven feet four and three-quarters inches— had measured. The chain went taut and wrenched the heavy leather collar around the Monk's neck, jerking it to a stop in mid-air, inches from Medici's face. The Monk dropped to the ground with a thump, its spunk and anger gone, a dazed expression on its face.

The sailors who watched said nothing for a moment, then one started to chuckle, then others laughed louder and louder. Medici stood looking down at the Monk who stared back dizzily. The laughter continued as Medici shook his head, dropped the two bananas in front of the Monk and walked back into the team house.

Ha Tien 1970

RATS

NWEEEEET! NWEEEEET! The high-pitched cry wakened Medici from his half sleep, terrified. His body was already tense as he slipped into full consciousness. The smell confirmed what his tired body already knew— rats!

Strange obsessions grip men in the combat zone. Medici's was rats. He hated the creatures with a passion that unnerved him when he thought about it rationally. The Indochinese version of the creature was the closest thing he had seen to the 1930's Disney cartoon rat— long wrinkled snout that wiggled brazenly in the air each time one appeared in his sleeping cubicle. But they were not cute. In fact, they were downright belligerent, often attacking their human enemies with shrill, shrieking violence that would scare them away.

But it was the smell that really got him. The dank musty, pungent smell of death that could permeate a room in seconds when a rat arrived through a drain hole of the dilapidated team house. Medici remembered the smell from his days climbing around the old well in his hometown, a huge brick cistern that had served for years as the town dump, held by local lore to contain rats larger than cats. It was only when he reached the Cambodian border that he discovered the smell was similar to that of decaying human flesh, but not as sweet.

The rats were aggressive enemies. Local war stories extolled their derring-do as they engaged Americans along the border. One gruesome tale involved a sleeping GI whose hand hung down to the floor next to a can of peanuts he had been eating before sleep. A rat, after gorging and emptying the can, mouthed the soldier's greasy, salty index finger to the second knuckle before the GI awakened, horrified, and flung it with a scream into the steel blades of the whirring paddle fan above. Undigested peanuts, rat feces and guts sprayed the room. These were tough bastards even in death.

Medici did not believe the lore. He had confidence he could destroy them all since as a child he had effectively exterminated a large and prolific family of field mice that had invaded his home one particularly cold winter. These tropical versions were just one more wily domestic enemy. He devised ways to lure them into the Asian version of a rat trap which the local blacksmith had provided. It consisted of an eighteen-inch-long chicken-wire cage with a spring-loaded trap door at one end, attached to a trigger mechanism that held the bait within the cage. Medici, when on an anti-rat jag, would fry up some pork fat from the market, bait the several cage traps within the house, then spend the evening waiting, as if on ambush, for the buggers to show up. The major disability of the traps was that they did not kill rats as the American snap-spring version did; they left the slaughter to the captor. In theory the entire trap *cum* rat was intended to be placed under water, and the rat drowned. But water was a scarce commodity on the team house hill, and it was too far and too dangerous to walk to the water's edge at night, so another method had to be devised.

Certain enlisted crazies like Bauer thought the answer simple: Shoot the fuckers with whatever was handy. But this solution freaked out the other occupants of the team house the first time he tried it at 3 A.M. The round ricocheted three times around the team house's plastered brick walls and through the woven bamboo partitions. No one was killed only because they were all prone on their bunks close to the floor. The Vietnamese Regional Forces who shared the hill started a firefight amongst themselves, fearing the compound was under sapper attack. The trap and rat were blown to smithereens.

Clearly, another method had to be found. They tried incinerating the rats with gasoline after capture, but that plan was abandoned because it was time consuming, wore out the wire traps and caused a horrendous smell. They had heard of an ingenious method used at Ben Tre, a province capital. An appropriate amount of Sakrete instant concrete was mixed with salty army canned cheddar cheese, then a mound of the mixture placed next to a large bowl of water. The rats would gorge on the cement-laced cheese during the night, drink their fill of water triggering the Sakrete. Dead, bloated rock-hard carcasses would be collected the next morning. But this was Ha Tien, the Barstow of Vietnam, and no Sakrete was available.

The final solution came from Medici, and it was an assassin's method. One night after the capture of a particularly obnoxious, squealing two pounder, he slipped into the major's office and quickly found the stiletto scissors of an elegant desk set given to the major by MACV commanders in Saigon. The rat, hungry and vicious, opened its snout and with long arched teeth attacked the thin point of the scissors, swallowing it two inches into its craw. Medici waited patiently for the rat to swallow and grasp it firmly. Then, while holding it vertically in the cage, he stabbed viciously down through its innards, twisting until he felt the spine snap and the rat quiver to a halt. He withdrew the scissors, wiped them with some toilet paper and returned them to the holder, hoping the major didn't use them for any personal grooming. He threw the rat's warm carcass out into the parking area in front of the team house where Dep, the rat-eating dog, quickly devoured it.

This procedure continued for several weeks with the major blissfully unaware of the use to which his scissors were put. Sgt. Duc, Medici's interpreter and driver, became increasingly uncomfortable with the slaughter of the rodents and, being a good Buddhist, told Medici it would bring bad karma. Medici told Duc he was raised Catholic and therefore feared God-directed lightning, not karma.

The slaughter was interrupted when Medici was sent on a mission. He was gone about three weeks and returned one afternoon to the Phao Dai team house, surprised how much the stinking place had become home sweet home for him. He unpacked his small bag and opened the top drawer of his dresser where he kept his bullets and medicine cabinet items received monthly in Red Cross care packages.

There he saw that a rat had viciously chewed through the box and aluminum foil of some EX-LAX. Why the Red Cross sent boxes of EX-LAX to Southeast Asia— rather like coals to Newcastle— mystified him. The rat had apparently mistaken its smell for chocolate and had eaten the entire contents of the two-inch square package. When Medici thought through the outcome he began to laugh out loud, thinking what a surprise the rat had later on. The laughter drew Sgt. Duc into the room, and he giggled like a small child about the consequences for the rat.

Medici opened the second drawer to replace some clean tee shirts and his laughter stopped abruptly. There, amidst the clean underwear where the same rat had nested in his absence, Medici stared with disgust at the precise location where the EX-LAX had taken effect on the rodent. Sgt. Duc peered into the drawer and giggled. Medici was at first furious, but Duc's mirth was so honest that Medici began to laugh again, this time at himself.

"See Dai-Uy, karma!" said Duc, eyes glistening.

"Karma," said Medici nodding his head in agreement, and the two of them walked to the patio to drink a beer in honor of the rat.

Ha Tien 1970

CALLING HOME

Medici awoke tired, hot and sweaty. Friday morning in Saigon, a Holy Day of Obligation, he remembered. The fetid air shone white, briefly spared the oily smoke of Honda-bikes while the Vietnamese elite attended mass at the Cathedral.

Medici ached with fatigue from yesterday's trip in from the border. It had taken seven hours to air-hike, first in a Huey, then two Air America Pilatus Porters. When he arrived at Tan Son Nhut Airport near midnight he was starved, and finding only the Dairy Bar open, drank a quart of chocolate milk. There he encountered a college classmate, the MACV historian, who found out Medici's job and said, "So you're the legendary NILO Ha Tien!" Medici walked away without comment.

By the time he reached the NILO crash pad in the Meyercord Hotel, he had hot painful diarrhea from the milk, which he could no longer digest. He fell into a troubled sleep at 3 A.M., and set his mental alarm for an early wakeup to line up at the USO for a call home before his noon briefing with Captain Ross.

He took a taxi for the short ride to the USO in light traffic through familiar Saigon streets. The Renault mini-cab bounced and jostled him, and his head throbbed when the driver stopped by careening into the curb.

"Bao nhieu tien?" *How much?* Medici asked.

"Nam muoi dong," *Fifty Piastres*, said the driver.

"No fuckin' way, asshole! Mac qua!" *Too expensive.* "Chi bon muoi dong!" *Only forty piastres!* Medici screamed, ready to tear the driver's head off.

"Okay, okay Dai-Uy. Forty Piastres okay," the driver said, wanting to get rid of the maniac. His expression told Medici he recognized these Americans who had been out in the boonies too long, the way they exploded from taciturnity to rage at the slightest provocation.

Medici gave him fifty piastres anyway, having won the dickering, then convulsed himself up and out of the tiny ramshackle Renault.

The USO building's gray stone facade distinguished it from a street of Chinese opticians' shops. Medici glanced at their windows, wondering if he should return to purchase rimless ovaloid French eyeglasses with gold frames, the kind worn by educated Vietnamese, and, in his mind's eye, complete his transformation from American officer to European expatriate.

He faced the USO door and wondered if his wife would be home. Twice before, after he waited in line for two hours, she was not home when the call went through. He felt his stomach twitch. He walked through the narrow wood and glass door up a narrower tile staircase. The landing opened to a pea-green room the size of a small lecture hall, already crammed with milling GIs.

A palpable air of tension gripped the room, like on night ambush. Its electricity surged through Medici and made his bowels roll. Each GI in the room feared the completion of his call— a breakthrough to "the world." Here, now, they could accept bullets, bombs and ambushes in the emotional vacuum they created for themselves in order to survive. But the dread of an unresponsive wife or girlfriend on the line, or news of a divorce proceeding, filled the air with the acrid odor of perspiration.

Medici walked to the varnished teak counter opposite mahogany and glass telephone booths which resembled confessionals. In the space between booths and counter stood rows of teakwood benches over which GIs in jungle fatigues flung themselves and waited for their turns, chain smoking, drumming their fingers, or biting their nails.

"Hi. I'm Lieutenant Medici and I'd like to call the States," he said to the American girl behind the counter. She was mousy haired and her eyes were too far apart, Medici thought. He wondered why he said Lieutenant instead of Tom.

"Well, hi! I'm Norma Smith. If you'll sign the list here we'll get your call out in twenty minutes or so. We've had clear circuits this morning. It's a good time to call."

Medici looked at her with a "No shit, Sherlock" look, but instead of saying anything acerbic, smiled faintly and said, "That's nice." He logged his wife's name and telephone number as the girl watched.

"Oh! A Cleveland number. Are you from Cleveland?" she asked. "I am!"

"No. Sorry. My wife's from there. She lives with her parents while I'm here," he answered, while his stomach churned.

The girl smiled, wrote his wife's name and number on a small rice paper slip and handed it to the headsetted operator to her left. "If you'll take a seat I'll call your name and direct you to a booth when the call goes through...." They both turned to see a commotion among the GIs at the entrance to the room.

An Army Public Affairs captain swept into the room gesturing dramatically with his arms. His actions telegraphed, "Make way, grunts, I've someone important with me." Medici watched with interest. The officer was obviously a staff puke from Saigon, and wore a tailored, starched green uniform, spit shined boots and captain bars of silver, not flat combat black. Asshole, Medici thought.

Medici turned round to the counter and Norma. He heard, "Hey, soldier. Make way for a Hollywood star. Come on, make a hole!" Medici planted his feet firmly. The captain pushed his way through the line to a spot at the counter next to Medici, leaned forward, spread his arms, and rested the fingers of one hand on the counter in front of Medici.

Medici stared at the hand. Without warning he spun a quarter turn and knocked the captain's hand from the counter, turning him to face Medici. GIs behind them guffawed.

"Oh, soddy!" Medici said with mock concern, his eyes drilling the captain's.

"Ec-excuse me," the captain stuttered, then returned to Norma.

Medici observed a tall, well-preserved man in his forties with carefully coiffed, silver-gray hair, Julius Caesar spit-curl style. The man smoked a cheroot as he eased his way to the counter through the annoyed GIs. Along the way he acknowledged comfortably greetings of GI fans as he passed, except that Medici noticed none of the GIs greeted or acknowledged him. They were simply pissed off that someone was pulling rank and cutting in front of them.

The captain was trying to persuade Norma to jump The Star to the head of the list to make an "important call" to Hollywood. She seemed unsure what to do. The Star gathered that the captain was getting nowhere, nudged him aside, beamed a radiant, seductive smile and extended his hand across the counter to Norma.

"Hi. I'm from Hollywood. You've probably seen me in *Breakfast at Tiffany's*," he whispered, taking her hand in both of his. "I'd like to make a call to L.A." he oozed, confident she would understand. His eyes remained fixed on hers, like a mongoose charming a cobra.

The girl gave the handsome man a broad smile, taken by his charm and attention. She blushed. The GIs watched in silence as The Star stared at her without blinking. Then they watched her lay her left hand on her breastbone, and flutter her eyelids. She withdrew her right hand from The Star's.

She tried to speak, but had to clear her throat first. She looked at him then said, "How do you do? I'm Norma Smith from Cleveland. If you'll sign the list here we'll get your call out in twenty minutes or so. We've had clear circuits to the States this morning...."

The Star looked down, began to fill out the form, then turned to a crescendo of applause and cheers. But he flushed when he heard "All right, Norma!" and "Atta girl, Norma!" from GIs all around the room. The Star completed the form, then sat on a middle bench with the captain to await his call amidst the happy GIs.

"Your turn, Mr. Medici. Booth one," a confident Norma said a few minutes later.

Medici smiled at her with appreciation, took his slip and walked toward the booth, wondering why Norma seemed a lot more attractive to him now than when he arrived.

Saigon 1970

SPECIAL WARFARE

JUNE 6, 1970

Medici read the white on blue Lexan sign "NAVSPECWARGRUV" on the ornate wood door. He had never been to this wing of the Naval Forces headquarters in Saigon, and it already had a different feel, a sense of danger. Commander Holland had told him to check in with Commander McQuillin, the SEAL Boss, at Special Warfare before Medici left for Sihanoukville, Cambodia on secret mission.

Medici rapped hard twice on the teak door. The door flew open and Medici faced an overly muscular lieutenant in jungle camo fatigues, with a black SEAL TEAM ONE VIETNAM patch sewn on his blouse. The lieutenant had close-cropped blonde hair, and bristled with hostility. Anomalously, he wore on a chain around his neck a circled inverted trident peace symbol. But on closer examination the trident bars spelled the word "WAR" in a trompe d'oeil.

"What do you want?" the SEAL demanded.

"Lieutenant Medici, NILO Ha Tien, to see Commander McQuillin. He is expecting me."

The lieutenant gave Medici a disdainful look and stepped aside to let him into the outer office. A large map of Vietnam, Cambodia and Laos covered the left wall, shaded windows the right. Straight ahead was another door to an inner office whose sign read "CDR McQuillin."

Medici scanned the outer office. A bristle-skulled yeoman sat at a wooden federal-issue desk typing a government form. Three other desks completed a box formation with the yeoman's. There was a tension in the air that Medici could sense, but not put his finger on.

"Butz, have you finished that after-action report about our My Tho mission," the lieutenant asked.

Butz responded without looking up from his typewriter. "Not yet sir. I'll be done in a minute."

"Make sure it comes out good." The lieutenant laughed. "Or I'll pummel your fat ass from here to Hong Kong." Medici noticed the last remark was spoken with a slight waiver in the lieutenant's voice. The lieutenant turned to Medici.

"Knock and go in, lieutenant," he said.

Medici approached the door, knocked and entered.

"Lieutenant Medici, NILO Ha Tien, reporting sir. Commander Holland sent me."

Commander McQuillin stood. He seemed old to Medici, at least 40, with a weathered ruddy face and an expression of fatigue. "Sit down, lieutenant," he said.

Medici sat in a wood-spoke office chair, the same as those in the outer office.

"So, you are going to Sihanoukville?"

"Yes, sir. I was called in from the border for the mission."

"You know, one of my guys wanted it." McQuillin raised his chin to point to the outer office. "They were pissed they'd give it to someone who wasn't Special Warfare."

Medici smiled and raised his palms. "What can I say, commander?"

McQuillin smiled. "Don't worry about it. Do you need any special weapons or support up there for the mission? I could send one of our guys as your bodyguard if you like."

"No thanks, commander. I'm used to traveling solo in strange places. My best protection is getting in and out alone before anybody knows I'm there. I usually don't tell anyone when I move on mission. Anyway, an extra guy will just slow me down, cause more talk and noise than going in solo. Thanks, anyway."

McQuillin laughed. "My guy won't like to hear that." He looked up. "Sure you won't need a weapon?"

"No, sir. I carry a Browning Hi-Power and a box of 9mm ammo wherever I go. And I may not be able to go in armed wearing civilian clothes. Doesn't look right."

McQuillin stroked his chin, then nodded. "Seems you thought this through…"

A shattering crash surged through the floor and rattled the office door. McQuillin jumped, ran to the door of the outer office and opened it.

Medici sat still, unperturbed. He turned and saw the SEAL lieutenant holding the yeoman by the lapels with his left hand, the typed report crumpled in his right, his face deep red. The lieutenant screamed, "You fucking moron! Don't you know this could get me kicked off the Teams?"

The yeoman looked petrified but remained silent. Medici observed the torn Indochina map, and two round holes in the plaster wall where the legs of a federal chair had penetrated.

"Lieutenant Danton, stand down!" McQuillin ordered.

Danton released the yeoman and turned away, punching his fist into his palm. McQuillin returned to his office and closed the door.

"See what I have to put up with? When my guys come in from the field for staff duty they become— well, a little frustrated."

Medici shrugged.

"Okay. Back to business. Is there anything you need?"

"Just the Leica camera gear and a lot of Pan-Ex film. Then I'll be on my way."

"Okay. The yeoman will get whatever you need. See you when you get back."

AUGUST 14, 1970

Commander McQuillin asked Medici to sit. The 24 year old looked five years older than when McQullin had last seen him, and it had only been nine weeks. His face was lined and drawn.

"Well, all's well that ends well. But did you have to shoot one of my guys?" McQuillin laughed.

Medici shrugged, then lifted his arms in supplication. He would never live this down. "You could have told me one of your guys was going on his own mission. I'd call that a conspicuous omission."

"Let bygones be bygones," McQuillin said, waving his hand. "You did a damn fine job up in Sihanoukville. I've seen the photography. The port survey information was first rate. You done good, m'boy."

Medici arched an eyebrow at "m'boy".

McQuillin sat. "Shut the door, lieutenant."

Medici stood and closed the door to the outer office where two officers and two enlisted men pretended not to overhear their conversation. Medici sat.

"You really did your mission fine, lieutenant. No fuss, no bother, no support, no problems with the natives. We like your style."

Medici wondered who "we" was. They sat in silence for a minute while McQuillin folded his hands.

"How would you like to be my X/O of Naval Special Warfare Group? It's a lieutenant commander's billet and will bring your second spot promotion in six months. I could use you."

Medici let out a slow breath. He was not expecting this. He was definitely on a fast career track if he took the job. But in an instant he flashed on Danton throwing the chair, and then on his own giddiness when General Lon Nol formally requested that he be appointed US Naval Attache to Phnom Penh. And the disappointment he felt when Washington sent a career officer instead. And the exhausting Board of Inquiry after Sihanoukville.

"Commander, I'm very flattered by the offer. But I am not SEAL or UDT trained. I'm not a killer-commando type. I'm a collection guy. That's what I do…"

McQuillin interrupted him. "Yes, but you can *think*. That's what I need here."

"Commander, I only have three months left in my tour, my second tour in Vietnam. I come from a family of lawyers and my sights are on law school as soon as my service is up. I am enormously honored that you would think of me to serve as your X/O. But I think I need to get to law school before I'm much older."

Medici stood. "Sorry, commander. I have to decline."

McQuillin raised his arms, palms up, in a "Wha'cha gonna do?" gesture. "Well, you know where to find me if you change your mind." He smiled.

Medici extended his hand and shook McQuillin's. Then walked out of Special Warfare forever.

Saigon 1970

18

A LITTLE HELP FOR MY FRIENDS

"I don't believe it!" Medici yelled, waving the yellow teletype paper wildly in front of Frank Brown. "Did you see this from our illustrious Commander-in-Chief, Richard M?"

"Yeah, NILO," Frank said. "He's got some balls, doesn't he?"

"He's been bombing Cambodia secretly for a year. Now we're supposed to make sure that we 'Do NOT repeat NOT provide ammunition or weapons to Cambodian forces during this critical period of review of U.S.-Cambodian relations.' This message is pure Kissinger playing Bismarck," Medici continued with slightly less steam.

"Yelling isn't going to help the Cambodes, NILO." Frank looked at him earnestly, trying to calm him down.

"You're right," Medici said quietly, meeting Frank's eyes for a moment. He crumbled the yellow "All Commands" message from the President, and tossed it swish-dunk into the radio room wastebasket on his way out the team house door.

Medici's spine hit with jarring thumps against the jeep's canvas seat each time it rolled over a rock or into the deep rut left by the monsoon. Despite the care with which he maneuvered the jeep, he seemed unable to avoid the bumps without lights in the moonless Asian night. The one-lane path stretched little more than half a kilometer from the top of the hill to the navy base below. In order to keep the noise down he used the clutch as a brake and covered in twelve minutes the distance he could do in three on foot. And his butt hurt like hell.

He reached the neck in the road where the base guard post stood, a stack of ammo cases with a sleepy sailor on top. High security, he thought. I can roll a jeep past this bozo. But the guard sat up and chambered a round in his M-16, letting Medici pass only after he said "NILO."

The jasmine smell of the Asian night was overwhelmed by diesel fumes of the oil applied to keep dust down around the helo pad. Medici edged slowly toward CONEX boxes of corrugated aluminum that served as the riverboats' armory. Redkin, a gunner's mate, sat slumped against a CONEX box on a grenade case, but stood up as the jeep crawled to a halt.

"Morning, Redkin."

"Yo, NILO! I mean LT. Medici. What's shakin'? It's zero three hundred." Brilliant radium numerals on Redkin's combat watch glowed visibly from three feet in the oily dark.

"Did I tell you my brother lives in Philly, Redkin? When I go to visit him we always go down to that cheese-steak place— what's it called?"

"Pat's. Oh, man, does that make my mouth water out here in the asshole of Veet Namb! Whatju doin' down here this hour of the night? I thought you spooks kept banker's hours."

"Nah, we're night people, Redkin. Don't you know how we got these jobs? Some dude from Naval Intelligence goes through the barracks at officers candidate school at three in the morning. Anybody up planning a gotcha gets to come to Nam as a Naval Intelligence Liaison Officer!"

Redkin laughed. "Some boot told me you was in nasal intelligence, 'cause of the size of your schnozz." Medici and Redkin snickered together; the gunner's mate was grateful for the banter on his mid-watch.

"Say, Redkin, you got any 60 mike-mike mortar rounds?" Medici said as casually as if it were the next jerky joke in their routine.

"What! What's a spy doin' with a 60 mm mortar?" Redkin said.

"Oh, we need it for protection on an op the army spook and I are doing tomorrow," he lied. "I need twelve cases, four high explosive, four illumination and four white phosphorous."

"Geez, NILO, you gonna start your own war? I'm accountable for this stuff. How come you didn't ask the C/O?"

"Hey, Redkin! I outrank your C/O," Medici parried, smiling. "Besides, the op just came up tonight and we have to leave early. How about two cases of each?"

"NILO, you pull more jive out here than any five guys I know," Redkin laughed, shaking his head. "Okay, but only six cases. I'll be in deep shit if I don't have enough for the boats. Where you want 'em?"

"In the jeep," Medici said as he headed into the dark CONEX box exactly to the spot where he had seen the 60 mm rounds earlier in the day.

At 10 A.M. through a nasty, light sleep Medici heard the unmistakable WHUP WHUP WHUP of a big helo. He bolted out of bed realizing he had overslept. He pulled on his madras shorts and flip-flops, then shuffled into the bright sun of the patio. He saw Frank Brown drinking a soda in one of the wooden easy chairs stenciled with ammunition markings. The helo circled the hill twice, its waxed and gleaming silver-blue sides suggested it was not Army. Medici held his hands high forming the football touchdown signal, and the pilot waved acknowledgement. Frank watched first Medici, then the chopper.

"Niiighlow," Frank said, recognition, then concern on his face.

"It's okay, Frank, believe me...."

"NIIIIGHLOW! It's probably a felony! In any case a court martial!" Frank was on his feet now trying to make himself heard over the chopper which passed overhead toward an unusual landing site, the far side of the hill from the navy base.

"Frank, it's okay, believe me," Medici said, pushing his palms toward him in a gesture of supplication. He backed off the patio then shuffled as casually as he could through the team house to avoid any further attention. As he went out the front door the major asked, "What's the Air America bird here for, NILO? I didn't know there were any CIA ops going on now."

"Don't know, Major, but I'll find out," he responded in his best Dudley Do-Right voice. He bounded down the steps, around the corner and out of sight to his hidden jeep, the cargo in its back seat covered with a moldy canvas tarp.

He roared across the parking area, hurling clouds of dust over the Vietnamese Ruffpuffs who had come out to see what the commotion was. Medici tore down the hill, heavy wooden cases crashing around the back seat as he flew over ruts and rocks. Medici, crazy with adrenalin, thinking about a court martial and naval prison, sang out loud against the din and crash, to the tune of "Shortening Bread":

Momma's little NILO gonna Portsmouth, Portsmouth,
Momma's little NILO gonna Portsmouth shed.
Momma's little NILO gonna Portsmouth, Portsmouth,
Momma's little NILO gonna end up dead!

At the foot of the hill he turned away from the navy base and bounced down the dirt road a kilometer to its junction with old French Route 8 that crossed into Cambodia. There, in the middle of the road, the Air America pilot touched down, unpitched his blades, and left the engine at high revs for quick takeoff. Medici drove off the road to the far side of the helo, to further obscure the view from the team house.

A lieutenant in navy fatigues jumped out. It was Niles, NILO at Chau Doc, next city east on the Cambodian border. He cupped his hands over Medici's ear to be heard over the helo whine.

"Did you see the All Commands message from the White House?" Niles asked.

Medici nodded.

"You still want to do it?" Niles continued.

"How did Sang Chit do last night?" Medici asked.

"Not well. NVA regulars kicked the hell out of the district compound. The Cambodes lost six more men. They can't even keep them away from the perimeter with those candy-ass carbines. They're gonna fold soon."

Sang Chit, Medici's Cambodian district chief friend, had for months during Cambodia's neutrality— and at great personal risk— provided them with good intelligence on NVA troop movements in his district that lay along the border. In the weeks since Prince

Sihanouk had been overthrown and while the White House was "re-evaluating" U.S.-Cambodian relations, the North Vietnamese quickly re-evaluated. They unmercifully hammered the outgunned Cambodian border districts to secure them as permanent infiltration corridors into South Vietnam.

"You sure you want to go ahead?" Niles asked.

"Fuck Nixon and his Kraut," Medici snorted. "Sang's a good dude. Let's load it."

Niles gestured to the pilot, and four Air America centurions in crisp white shirts, Saigon mirror sunglasses and heavy gold bracelets jumped out, all tanned and smiling like a toothpaste commercial. They each grabbed a case of the mortar ammo and loaded it into the helo. Medici and Niles followed with the last two.

"Say hello to Sang and give him this," Medici yelled into Niles' ear and slapped the shiny new April 1970 *Playboy* onto his lap. "An unknowing gift from the major," he laughed.

Medici backed away as the pilot began to pull pitch on the big blades. He looked at the shining aircraft, then the crew, shook his head in disbelief and shouted, "Simonized helicopters— SHEEE-IT!" They grinned back, lifted off, and were gone.

Ha Tien 1970

MOTORING TO TAN CHAU

"Tom. Can you meet me in Chau Doc and drive with me to Tan Chau over on the Mekong? We've got some disturbing reports I'd like to verify and I may need your French to communicate with these guys."

Medici could barely hear Jack Hendrick's voice on the scratchy field telephone circuit. Jack was the Fourth Riverine Area Intelligence Officer, technically not in Medici's chain of command, but a good dude. Besides being smart, polite and helpful, he had put Medici in for an award for his secret weapons negotiation with the Cambodian government in the days preceding the incursion, when Medici's own boss, the Walrus, hadn't lifted a finger for him. Medici owed Jack one.

"Sure, Jack. When should I be there?" Medici shouted into the mildew-smelling handset.

"Any time the next day or two. See you at Niles."

"Roger, at Niles— WORKING"— he shouted at another voice that had come on the common army telephone circuit. "See you soon."

The swingship didn't come for two days. Why, no one knew. But on the third day a Chinook helicopter dropped down on the Ha Tien pad to deliver a pallet of soft drinks, and Medici persuaded the pilot to take him to Chau Doc on the way back to the big airbase at Can Tho.

They flew over the tram forest to intercept the Vinh Te Canal, then paralleled it at a safe distance one click to the south to its intersection with the Bassac River, exactly where Chau Doc sat. They landed in the flat field that surrounded an old French fortress that looked like Carcasonne, not so much because of its shape, but because of the burnt color of the bricks, a soft, deep rust brown that from a distance gave the illusion of velvet.

He half expected a drawbridge to be lowered to let him in, though there was no moat. Instead, a stockade door of logs greeted him, manned by two young Americans in army fatigues, one without front teeth. He didn't identify himself, but walked straight past their half-hearted waves. He turned to ask where he could find Lieutenant Niles Chitwood, NILO Chau Doc, and they pointed to the top floor of the fortress.

He trundled up the long flights of worn brick steps until he reached the top floor where a cool breeze chilled him as it blew through empty window frames. The place was like a dungeon. He traveled halfway around the perimeter hallway and poked his head in the first doorway. There, on a bunk bed made of log posts, lay Niles Chitwood, NILO Chau Doc. His left leg was elevated, the calf heavily bandaged and splinted. Jack Hendrick sat on a rust covered bridge chair, drinking a beer.

"Niles, What Happened!"

"Saigon. I was back at headquarters for debriefing. I'm walking back through the park on my way to the Meyercord. Right next to the Cercle Sportif, five-thirty in the afternoon in bright sunlight we get a goddam rocket attack. Big Soviet 122s come slamming in. It looked like D-Day.

"The first one hit the Cercle and took out a tennis court. I hit the ground, but the next one detonated in the trees, spraying shrapnel like an airburst. I was lucky; a half-inch sliver pierced my leg and chipped the bone. A four-inch chunk drove two feet into the grass next to my head. I could feel the heat from it as it went by.

"Apparently the occasion for the attack was some Buddhist holiday. So much for the pleasures of the city! I've been NILO out here for eighteen months without a scratch, but I get my Purple Heart in the park in Saigon." Niles laughed.

Medici turned to Jack, "Guess Niles isn't going anywhere for awhile. It's you and me to Tan Chau, eh?"

"Niles gave us his jeep and grenade launcher for the trip. We'll be taking along a Vietnamese interpreter and escorting two North

Vietnamese soldiers captured yesterday. They're from the 9th North Vietnamese Division and are on their way to the interrogation center at Can Tho. Air America will pick them up at Tan Chau."

"You lazy fuck," Medici said to Niles, who drank a beer. "Anything to get out of a pleasant drive through the countryside!" They both laughed, because they knew it wasn't true.

"Tom, drive slow and watch the road carefully. There have been a number of minings lately, and it isn't all that secure. Leave mid-morning so the South Vietnamese Army will have completed their morning mine sweep. You should arrive mid-afternoon, what with the ferries and all."

Niles spoke this information in what seemed to Jack to be an unduly serious, quiet tone. But Medici understood exactly that the shift in tone was a jump from banter to the transfer of serious operational information from one field agent to another. This was a special wavelength on which good field agents spoke to each other. The change of tone could come at any time, and it demanded immediate, rapt attention.

"Are they command-detonated or contact mines?" Medici asked.

"Both. Just keep your eyes peeled and drive slow. I've filled the floor of the jeep with sandbags. That should give you a little protection for all but a direct hit."

Jack was amazed at the non-verbal communication between these two NILOs. As an administrative intelligence boss, he seldom needed the field smarts these guys did. Now he had the feeling of watching two deadly animals backed in a corner with their hackles up against a common enemy. He could feel rather than see or hear the animal fear and cunning that underlay their discussion. He was glad they were on his side and was proud to work with guys like this, two Ivy Leaguers who did not have to be out here on the border by themselves. They could be in Saigon or Canada, or avoid service with a false excuse from a family doctor.

A career naval officer, Jack hoped they could retain young men like these after Vietnam was over. But his guess was guys like these two would never be satisfied with the peacetime navy. If they stayed, their next billets would likely be some intelligence office in the Pentagon or with a carrier air wing. B-O-R-I-N-G. Hendrick had done it himself. The really good ones seldom stay, he thought.

But these guys, after a NILO job at twenty-four, would probably never be satisfied with anything conventional that civilian life had to offer. His guess was Niles would go to business school and work for some international corporation because of his family background— half-French, half-American— and a Harvard education.

Medici was a tough little wop who was exasperatingly analytical, probably the result of a rigorous Jesuit high school education of Augustinian logic and debate. Definite lawyer candidate. They would both probably start with big firms until the impact of this NILO tour caught up with them. They would be bored, disillusioned that none of their peers and superiors worked with the fervor or discipline or willingness to take risks that they did. Then they would quit in a funk, brood by themselves for a while, and strike out on their own, perhaps together, to continue with NILO esprit in real life— brash and self-confident.

But loners after all. It was a loner's job, and there were no two ways about it. Strange breed, he thought. It amazed him how self-selecting the job was, and how the right people found out about it and gravitated to it. One of life's small mysteries.

'Wonderful,' Medici thought. How do I get into these little side trips that happen to be filled with physical risk. I'm too short for this, only three months left. Why can't I just stay in Ha Tien and review reports until I'm sent home. Well, I volunteered for it....

"Grab a beer, Tom, and we'll go down for chow. I'll need help down the stairs," Niles said. "Bunk here tonight and you can leave in the morning after they sweep Route 53 on the other side of the Bassac.

They watched the ARVN minesweepers rumble down Route 53 for the morning sweep. The Bassac was only two hundred yards wide near the fortress and from Niles' third floor window they saw the diesel trucks start with oily black puffs of smoke, then chug noisily down the road. Mine sensing gear protruded like a beetle's antennae in front of the first truck.

Medici scratched himself then pulled on his jungle greens. Jack and Niles were already up. Jack had showered and shaved and looked Saigon spiffy. Niles hobbled around in jungle green trousers from which one leg had been cut away for his splint and bandages. Neither he nor Medici showered or shaved. This was a mission day. Neither smiled or chatted with Jack or each other. All communications were short and pertained to the route they would take to Tan Chau, where they could safely stop, and what to watch for. It made Jack nervous but he kept silent.

They quickly ate a breakfast of dehydrated eggs and fresh pineapple, and abominable army coffee. Niles led them outside where his navy jeep was fueled and ready at the stockade gate. Manacled and chained in the back seat were two fifteen-year-old North Vietnamese soldiers, the youngest Medici had seen. They wore gray uniforms without insignia, and high-top gray canvas battle sneakers that had carried them down the Ho Chi Minh trail. They looked like a pair of hapless geeks, so estranged from their environment that they seemed to float. And they were scared witless.

Leering in the front seat was a puffy, cologned Vietnamese in pointy black shoes with a shiny new M-16 across his lap. He smoked a Marlboro that hung languidly from his lip. Niles introduced him as Mung, the colonel's personal interpreter and driver who was charged with escorting the NVA prisoners to Tan Chau.

Medici disliked him instantly. The guy reeked of the privilege that comes from ingratiating oneself to the occupying forces. He had black market written all over him from the cologne, to the cigarettes, to the ostentatious gold ring, bracelet and chain that he wore. Mung saluted, then reached to shake their hands and Medici noticed his nails were manicured. Manicured!! In the middle of the fucking Vietnam War. Medici grimaced.

"Let's go," Medici said to Mung, his lips drawn tight. Mung turned in the driver's seat and started the engine.

"No, I'll drive," Medici said and motioned a bewildered Jack Hendrick into the passenger seat. He motioned Mung into the back with the NVA boys, who stared with their mouths open. Medici pushed them gently over to one side so Mung had room. Mung sat against the rear corner of the jeep, half hung out, so he could keep his rifle trained on the cowering two. Medici sat at the wheel and they departed.

The main ferry, diesel driven, was out of service. A VC mine had destroyed it two nights before. They were sent down the river a half click to the alternate ferry, a Huck Finn float guided across by a rope and powered by a 1947 Evinrude outboard motor that sputtered and spewed oily blue smoke that made them nauseous.

They had to get out of the jeep and position their weight according to the grunted instructions of the ferryman in order to level the raft and cock it properly into the current. Mung got very nervous trying to keep his rifle trained on the two NVA and still keep his balance, and they laughed when he almost went over backwards into the Bassac.

Downriver, even this close to Chau Doc, purse nets dotted both banks, each like a large wire wok ladle. Weirs, maze-like fish traps supported by stakes, paralleled long sections of the riverbank except in the ferry channel. Vietnamese peasants, languid and expressionless, stood in twos and threes on the bank, waiting for their turn on the ferry.

Medici drove the jeep carefully off the raft onto the bank and two peasants led a large ox onto the raft. It panicked, shuffled around the tippy platform, then dumped the peasants, ferryman, and itself into the muddy brown river to the laughter of the spectators on the bank.

The paved road along the river led them north through the hamlet of Chau Giang, directly across the river from Chau Doc, then northeast onto Route 53 across the paddies toward Tan Chau. The way was clear of obstructions save an occasional army checkpoint and several mine-blown holes in the dike road that required them to detour in four-wheel drive down the face of the dike then up onto the road. The day grew oppressively hot and the sky sank lower, laden with humidity, filtering the light to leaden gray.

Medici grew fidgety. He stopped several times so he could urinate. He climbed down the dike bank feeling weak, believing that snipers were focusing their telescopic sights on him, and noted detachedly that his urine was dark yellow, then root beer brown when his bladder was almost empty. He worked his way back up to the road and noticed that for the third time Mung was screaming evilly at the North Vietnamese boys. He wished they had not taken Mung and the prisoners.

They drove further and it grew hotter. The stifling humidity made it hard for Medici to breathe. They stopped at a solitary roadside palapa with an ancient Waring blender powered by a car battery. With ice, tropical fruits and sugared condensed milk the owner concocted frappes. Medici bought for all of them, including the boys, which Mung showed by his facial expressions to be an unforgivable breach of war etiquette.

Medici felt better after the cool drink, but the road beyond the stand was full of potholes, some unpatched. The jeep's suspension was hard and the going was slow. They rocked and banged inside the jeep as Medici maneuvered as best he could between the holes. Soon, a Vietnamese army half-track roared up behind them with a clanking whine, then laid on its klaxon forcing Medici to pull over to let it by. The soldiers on board were drunk and threw empty 33 Export beer bottles over the jeep into the paddies, laughing as they went. They roared down the road ahead of the jeep, the steel tracks clanking and bucking over the potholes. "Cowboys," Medici said to Jack.

The half-track sped around a short curve in the road two hundred yards ahead of them, then drove up an imaginary incline, looped-the-loop and fell back on itself in a huge cloud of dirt and black smoke. It crashed and bounced upside down, then slid off the edge of the dike road spilling cowboys in every direction. The concussion reached the jeep before the thump-roar of the mine's explosion.

Medici stopped and they jumped out. He scanned the tree line to their right and saw two men in black pajamas carrying AKs running crouched into the trees. He loaded a round into the grenade launcher and fired it in their direction. The first round landed short. The second caused one VC to drop his AK, but both disappeared into the trees.

Jack drove and Medici rode shotgun with the launcher. The dust settled as Jack maneuvered cautiously forward in the jeep. Now they could hear wailing Vietnamese soldiers, some missing arms or hands, some only shell-shocked. The inverted half-track smoldered, tracks still turning. They saw limbs extending from under the cab, twitching involuntarily. A wake of foaming 33 Export beer bottles stood between the jeep and the half-track. A Vietnamese officer, only slightly wounded, recovered his senses and shouted shrilly in Vietnamese over his field radio. He motioned Medici and Jack on with violent waves of his good arm, making it clear he did not want any help from the Americans.

Medici was nauseous. How much more of this did he have to endure? There might be another command-detonated mine in any one of these potholes along the way. Jack was silent.

The boy soldiers were as scared as the rest of them. Their patriotism was not so deep that they wanted to die at the hands of a Viet Cong mine squad for the glory of Ho Chi Minh. For the first time during the trip, one whispered something to the other as Jack drove away from the half-track. Mung cursed and struggled with his M-16. He screamed at the boys to stop whispering, chambered a round in the rifle, and jammed the flash suppressor into the whisperer's cheek, abrading his skin and making him gag. Mung shouted with fury for another ten seconds.

Medici signaled Jack to stop. He turned around, withdrew the Browning, pulled back the hammer to full cock and stuck it in Mung's cheek just as Mung had done to the prisoner.

"Put the rifle down and put the safety on, Mung," he said. He stared at Mung who looked at him incredulously. "NOW!" Medici screamed so loudly he startled himself.

Mung was more humiliated than scared. He had lost his authority in front of the prisoners. He lowered the rifle, put it on safe, and stood it on the floor of the back seat.

Medici took the rifle, slid it in the front next to the grenade launcher, half-cocked the pistol, and slid it back in his waistband. He told Mung to sit fully in the back seat next to the boys. Mung complied without protest, not hate but indifference in his eyes. Now there were three prisoners.

The last five kilometers were quiet and uneventful, the tension of the mining relieved by the Mung episode. Small groups of hooches appeared as they approached the Mekong end of Route 53. They came to the interrogation center and stopped to discharge Mung and the prisoners. Medici gave Mung back his rifle. Mung put the strap over his shoulder and gestured the boys inside to God knew what fate, Medici thought. Medici switched with Jack and drove the half mile to the French dam and flood control station that straddled a narrow neck of the Mekong. The building was crisp white stucco with royal blue trim.

They parked the jeep and walked up the concrete levee steps to the upriver side of the floodgate. Jack leapt ahead of Medici, taking the small steps three at a time. When Medici reached the top Jack was standing there, hands hanging at his side, staring at the huge dipstick and floating pointer that showed the Mekong's depth. It read six meters. Medici looked at the blank expression on Jack's face, puzzled why the river's depth could have that effect on him.

Then his eyes followed the dipstick to the water line and again he felt the nausea. Bloated bodies lay rafted around the dipstick along the floodgate wall, and upriver fifty yards. There were scores of bodies, the air curiously devoid of the sickening sweet smell, he thought. He noticed crabs crawling and nibbling on the closest corpses. Small birds jumped from corpse to corpse, pecking on a bursting chest here, a cheek there. The swollen river was a rusty brown as far as the eye could see, not the light brown of monsoon season. Bloated islands of flesh bobbed here and there upriver to the bend.

Jack turned slowly to Medici. "The Cambodes are slaughtering all the ethnic Vietnamese in the border and river towns, ostensibly purifying the population to insure political loyalty. Their new enemy is the Vietnamese since Cambodia entered the war on our side. They just have trouble differentiating between North Vietnamese and South Vietnamese." He paused and laughed a black laugh. "I guess from their standpoint the only good Vietnamese is a dead Vietnamese, politics notwithstanding."

They decided to leave the jeep and fly back by helo. On the short flight back to Chau Doc, Medici repeated for Jack the puzzling story Cambodian Governor Um Samuth had told him with tears of laughter in his eyes when Medici had first met him. Bursting with ethnic pride, Samuth told Medici that the last time Cambodia had gone against the "Vietnamese aggressors," they had captured the three top generals, buried them up to their heads and built small sandalwood tea fires around each head. A teapot was boiled on each and tea was served while the Cambodian generals sat and chatted in a circle around the conquered generals, now serving their Cambodian captors so humiliatingly.

"When was that?" Medici asked.

"Around 1208." said Samuth.

Medici had not understood Samuth's humor at the time, nor believed the extraordinary cultural antipathy and barbarism that lurked just below the surface in these outwardly gentle Cambodians. At Tan Chau he understood.

Ha Tien 1970

RALPH

"Old Joe Kennedy was right. They should walk down the halls of the State Department and fire every other son of a bitch. They're all a bunch of foreign policy phonies. I've been there, I know," Ralph Lombardi said. I could not disagree with him.

Ralph plays a good piano at the Viet-My bar on Saigon's Thai Lap Thanh Street. In his off time, that is. During daylight, he lectures on "American Civilization" at Saigon University, and has for thirteen years.

Ralph came to Saigon in 1962 on a trip to the Orient calculated to broaden his personal philosophy. He had just taken a degree at Oxford in foreign affairs after two earlier diplomas from Harvard and Columbia. Not bad for a kid from Brooklyn, he says. His stints with the National Security Council staff and the Council on Foreign Relations convinced him he needed time off for detached thought, away from the establishment. Ralph sensed something wrong in the American approach to foreign policy. He arrived to identify what the failing was. Saigon in 1962 was a city of fifteen thousand Frenchwomen, oriental mystique, an occasional Foreign Legionnaire, and few bungling Americans. It enchanted Ralph. He stayed.

Ralph tells me stories about characters he has known when I sit and listen to him play, whenever I return to Saigon from my post on the Cambodian border.

Ralph continued. "…Cabot Lodge was one of the good ones. He used to come and sit right over there to hear me play. Not just the rinky-dink stuff I do to keep customers, but Malaguena and Rachmaninoff concertos and other pieces hard for the untrained ear to listen to.

"I remember one night back in the beginning, Lodge was here with a bunch of sycophants from his embassy staff. They clung to him like lampreys, each forcefully and earnestly urging on him their solutions to the growing war. After a while he broke free and came to the piano. He looked gray and drawn, like he hadn't had a good night's sleep in weeks. He said to me 'Ralph, I know you're an expert in foreign affairs and I've heard about your degrees and all that. I'm surrounded by these so-called experts all day long. They each try to tell me what to do about the guerrilla problem and the corruption of Diem's government. And none of them are right. Ralph, you play a damn good piano and never try to tell me what to do.... Keep playing, Ralph.' At that, Lodge gave me a little pat on the shoulder, and started back toward the group, staring at the floor in front of him as he walked. That was in summer '63. We killed Diem, and you know how it went after that."

The Viet-My closes around 2 a.m. and despite the curfew there are always hangers-on. Guys like me from the boonies, tense, exhausted, gaunt and secretly confused by what we saw each day in the field. It occurred to me that I was hanging on just barely when I sloshed the last Martell on the blouse of my musty nine-day cammies.

I threw a pocketful of dirty piastres on the table without counting and got up to leave, then thought to ask Ralph, through a cognac fog, "Why are you here, doing this all these years?"

He turned to me, kept playing, and said, "Because they're mostly phonies, and this is kind of my vigil, y'know?"

"Yeah, I know," I replied sullenly, not really understanding, and walked into the sandalwood scented night to face the tinny roar of a thousand Honda-bikes.

Saigon 1970

DAI-UY HUNG'S ICE CREAM PARLOR

"Duc-aye!" Medici called into his interpreter's quarters. Co Hoan glided out of Sgt. Duc's room to her room next door, buttoning her silk blouse. She averted her eyes from Medici's.

"Dai-Uy?" Duc beamed a radiant, sleepy smile, buttoning his green fatigue shirt.

"It's hot, Duc. How about some ice cream before the DIOCC meeting?"

"Da phai, dai-uy!"

"I thought we could go to Dai-Uy Hung's for *crème glacee*."

"OK, Dai-Uy." Duc's smile was contagious, and put Medici in a good mood. Besides his military and language talents, Duc's goodwill and buoyant spirits were what Medici valued most.

They jolted down the hill in Medici's Jeep, Duc driving. He rolled carefully over the sharp rocks which protruded from the hardened mud wheel ruts. Medici braced his right foot against the Jeep's door cut, his left foot on the sandbags which lined the footwell for mine protection, his right hand on the dash grab bar, his left holding his rifle across his lap. They reached the bottom of the hill, drove past the graveyard, glanced at each other quickly, each gauging the other's pain at the memory of the loss of the orphan Em Chau who rested there. They gained speed on the straight away lined with bales of rotting fish, the beginnings of nuoc mam fish sauce. The smell in the hot August sun followed them for blocks beyond the bales.

They turned down the street of the National Police Headquarters at Ha Tien. Medici and Duc saw the District Chief's Jeep parked in front, two hours early for the DIOCC meeting.

"Dai-uy, I will find out what is going on there. I think they should be telling you, and not meeting alone," Duc said cautiously. Medici simply nodded, and wondered what was up. Rumor of attack or assassination?

"Later, Duc. Let's get some ice cream now."

Duc turned off the blacktop on to a rouge dirt side street and stopped the Jeep in front of a ten foot wide space between two white stucco buildings. A wide banyan tree formed the back wall of the tiny space, which was shaded by a white military parachute, suspended like a tent by five of its cords on some rebar and sticks. The parachute covered a brushed dirt circle on which stood, improbably, two white marble belle époque bistro tables with elaborate, green bronze curlicue legs, brought originally from some long gone Paris café. Two strings of white pinpoint lights were strung under the parachute, and were lighted at night with a small generator powered by a boy pedaling a bicycle without a rear wheel. Wooden grenade cases stood on end and served as chairs for each table. Medici always laughed at the clever resourcefulness of the Vietnamese to cobble together an ice cream parlour here in the Barstow of Vietnam.

They sat at a table. The parachute actually helped keep the parlour cool in the hot sun, or at least suggested the illusion of cool and calm. Medici leaned his M-16 against the tree— no one could get behind him here.

As if from nowhere, a very young girl appeared from around the corner of one building and greeted them shyly.

"You have ice cream today?" Duc asked.

"*Nous l'avons,*" she replied.

"What flavor?"

"*Rhum raisin,*" she said, pronouncing it "Rhoom ray-sann."

Duc looked at Medici who shrugged, then nodded.

"*Deux, s'il vous plait,*" Duc said to her, and smiled.

The girl giggled and smiled back at Duc, then shuffled around the corner. Duc always has a way with the ladies, Medici thought.

Duc and Medici eyed the street. There was no one about in the hot afternoon sun. Waves of heat shimmered from the red dirt and the roofs of small Vietnamese houses across the street.

"Duc— it's too quiet," Medici said, lifting his rifle to his lap.

"Maybe, Dai-uy." Duc smiled, stood, walked to the street, and looked both ways as a Vespa putted around the corner driven by a young man in plastic sandals, brown pants, beige shirt, and a jazz musician's fedora. He drove right toward Duc, then veered off and lobbed a grenade past Duc at Medici's feet. Duc drew his .45, and with his first shot, blew the man's head apart as he putted away. The Vespa tumbled in a red spray of brain matter onto the rouge street, its motor running, wheels still spinning.

Medici sat, agape at the cylindrical Chinese grenade. He noticed its texture actually looked like a pineapple with its crude cast shrapnel scorings. There was nowhere to go— not back into the banyan, not around the corner, not behind a table. He could hear the grenade's fuse sputtering, and watched it emit a little spurt of gray smoke. He knew he was dead.

The grenade paused, made one last sputter, and lay dormant.

Medici was thinking of his wife, his mother, how stupid he was to volunteer for Vietnam and the Cambodian Border. He had thought himself into a floating state of narcosis, hoping to numb the pain of the blast. It took him half a minute, then another, to realize the grenade was a dud.

Ha Tien 1970

39

Kaoh Pou Island
Pirate Islands
Cambodia

Beach Palms

West Lagoon

Sandy Beach

Mangroves

Triple Canopy Jungle

+ 190 ft.

Ridgeline

East Cove

Extraction Point

PIRATE ISLANDS, CAMBODIA

The field telephone in the hospital had crusted blood on it, making Medici wince. On it he could barely hear Lieutenant John Nelson Ferrara:

"Tom! What's the matter with you? We need our NILO up here," John shouted.

"They say I've got infectious hepatitis. Probably from eating some bottom feeder shellfish in Cambodia. How do you like that? NVA, VC and Khmer Rouge can't catch me, but this damn bug does!"

"Tom, I had it two years ago. It's 4-6 months recovery. I think your tour is over." John paused. "I regret we still haven't done the Pirate Islands op."

"You're right, John. Doc says I can't go back to Ha Tien, I'm too contagious. They're medevacing me out to Japan tomorrow."

Medici remembered his longing to catch the coastal infiltration junks moving communist supplies to the VC from Cambodia. His agent net reported big, motored sampans heading south along the coast at night. They hid in the sampan fishing fleets off each fishing town until they received the 'All Clear" light signal to proceed further south flashed by VC sympathizers in the hills along the coast. Once the big sampans knew the coast was clear of US and Vietnamese patrol craft, they would head south to the next cluster of fishing boats to await the next all clear signal. The Cambodian Pirate Islands, straddling the border between Cambodia and Vietnam eight miles off the coast, offered an ideal location from which to watch this enemy activity, or to capture enemy who used the island for infiltration.

"Damn, what a way to leave." John paused again. "Listen, Tom. Tan and I are ready to go. May we borrow your shortwave SSB radio for the Pirate Islands operation?"

"Of course. Tell the Major I said it's okay. It's stored in the rafters of Duc's quarters at the compound on Phao Dai." Exhausted as he was, Medici felt himself slip into NILO mode.

"Look, John, if you go to the islands, use at least two men with adequate fire power. Have a cover PBR and the Seawolves ready to scramble. If you hit a big gang of VC moving weapons in a heavy sampan they'll have a lot of fire power. Don't go in if you see any daytime activity on the island, fishermen or whatever— WORKING!!" Medici yelled as a whiney army colonel came on the party line. The colonel hung up.

"You'll probably want to go to Kaoh Pou, the northernmost large island. It has a hill about 190 feet above sea level, and if you station up top— and there are no VC there already— you will be able to view the whole coast from Kep, Cambodia to Ha Tien, and see any flashing light signals they may be using for 'All Clear' to direct their motor sampans south.

"Tread lightly John. Back-up will take longer than you can probably hold out if it's bad." Medici paused, shook his head and said "Shit, I wish I was going with you."

Lieutenant Ferrara and Trung Uy Tan of Coastal Group 43 ate an early dinner and surveyed their gear. The NILO's shortwave radio was too bulky and heavy to take to Kaoh Pou island, so they took a PRC-77 tactical radio with a long tape-measure antenna. Near the top of Kaoh Pou's 190 foot hill they would be able to contact the tactical operations center at Ha Tien, which could scramble Seawolf helos at To Chau across the river, and directly alert the back-up PBR standing off the island. As a practical matter, the Hueys could not reach the island for 20-30 minutes. At 26 knots on a calm Gulf the cover PBR would arrive in minutes for back-up or extraction.

Confident and prepared, LT Ferrara and Trung Uy Tan sat on the porch at the Phao Dai team house and surveyed the Gulf with binoculars waiting for the 2300 nighttime departure.

LT Ferrara and Trung-Uy Tan

At 2245 hours they loaded their gear aboard the lead PBR: the PRC-77, big navy 7x50 bridge binoculars, two M-16s, a scoped .308 Winchester M70 rifle, hand grenades and an M79 grenade launcher with fat high explosive, flechette and white phosphorus rounds. If they made contact with the enemy and the shit hit the fan, the M79 and hand grenades were key to survival given the island's cover. LT Ferrara carried the 9mm Belgian Browning pistol Medici had gifted him.

PBR 116 was commanded tonight by LTjg Jerry Marsden. Jerry had come to Ha Tien from the ill-faded destroyer *USS Frank E. Evans*, and had been junior officer of the deck when the Australian aircraft carrier *HMAS Melbourne* sliced the smaller ship in half during a botched stationing maneuver. In the best naval tradition, the crew of the bad luck ship was scattered to the four winds. After training, Jerry was sent directly to Ha Tien as a PBR patrol officer. Despite the *Evans* mishap, not Jerry's fault, Jerry was a fine patrol officer and John and Tan were glad to have him tonight for insertion, extraction and possible fire support.

The Gulf of Thailand was silky calm to the horizon as they eased quietly out of Ha Tien Bay, the cover boat following a mile behind, hoping not to alarm VC watchers who could compromise their mission. They idled out for three miles to keep the engine noise down, then slowly increased speed as they pulled further offshore. There they encountered a short slick swell, so they could not plane the PBR at full speed to Kaoh Pou, but pressed ahead at 16 knots to the island.

Marsden slowed the PBR when the silhouette of the island was in sight. The big GMC diesels purred and sputtered as they dropped in and out of idle.

"Where's the best place to land, John? Still the west lagoon beach, like we discussed?" Marsden said, shining a red flashlight on the chart.

"Yes, the west lagoon beach. The tide is mid-high, coming in, so at slow speed you should be able to put us on the south end of the beach close to the base of the hill."

"Okay. Looks good. Again— just in case— same emergency

extraction point, we discussed? You know, if you have to get out of there quickly." He turned to Ferrara to make sure they were both in agreement, shifting his weight from one foot to the other.

Ferrara nodded. "ROGER, Jerry. Got it. I still think the southerly tip of the island is the best place for escape to the water. There's a long ridge line from the top of the hill to a small cliff which drops down to deep water at all tides. Tan and I reconned it last month. If we have to *didi mau* we can move quickly down the ridge line, leap off the cliff into the water, and you can give us covering fire and pull us out."

"ROGER that. You have a man overboard light, right?"

"Right here." Ferrara covered the light with his hand and flicked it on. It glowed pink through the flesh of his hand and did not harm their night vision.

The PBR purred slowly around the south point of Kaoh Pou. The cover boat stood off dark and silent two miles out. Marsden's crew had their guns ready and bearing, while Ferrara, Marsden and Tan scoured the hillside with binoculars for muzzle flashes or any activity. They saw none.

Marsden spoke quietly to the bow gunner, BM3 Thompson, who had brought a jury-rigged lead line.

"Tommy, slide the line quietly over the side— no splash— readings every 30 seconds or so. Tell me when we reach five feet of water."

"Aye," whispered Thompson.

Even in the gloom of the moonless night they could see clearly the white sand of the west beach, and the green tropical phosphorescence where the waves broke. When the boat was 150 yards from shore the swell began to rise against the bottom. At 40 yards Tommy whispered "Five feet."

Marsden backed the diesels to slow their forward progress.

"I'll have to put you in wet, John. I don't think I can beach and back off in these shallows. I can't afford to lose another ship." Marsden laughed. "Will you guys be okay with all that gear?"

"Tan and I are carrying 50 pounds each and critical comm gear. How about you drop a kedge anchor astern so you can pull her off?

I'd like to get in shallower water so we don't drown the radio. It's our only connection to you and the cover boat once we are on the jungle floor and climbing— if we need emergency extraction."

Marsden nodded, ducked below and emerged with a double-fluked stockless anchor and 150 feet of nylon line from a compartment. He quickly flaked the line so it would run free, then heaved the anchor smartly over the stern. By playing the line he set the anchor so it held.

The aft gunner tended the line around the mounting post of his .50 caliber as the PBR eased forward in the gentle swell toward the beach.

"Three feet… two feet," Thompson said.

"Tie her off," Marsden said to the aft gunner. The PBR held in the shallows, gently hobby-horsing in the swell. "Ready John?"

Ferrara nodded. Tan held the PRC-77 radio above his head to keep it out of the water as the two slid from the bow into two feet of warm Gulf water.

"See you later, alligator," Ferrara said. He heard Marsden laugh.

"See you at 0700 extraction— if not before," Marsden whispered. He slowly backed the PBR away from the shallow west beach as his stern gunner retrieved the line and anchor. Then the PBR was gone from sight.

Ferrara and Tan waded ashore and quickly headed south off the beach to the cover of the heavy palms at the foot of the hill. The glowing hands of his military watch showed exactly 2400 hours, midnight— the witching hour. They moved further south and encountered heavy mangrove at the end of the beach, so they turned southwest toward the base of the hill, up and over a first low ridge, then into black, dark, double and triple canopy jungle.

"Good thing we reconned this hill in daylight last month, Tan. It would be nearly impossible going if we hit this cold." Tan grunted as he tightened the radio straps so he could hold his flechette-loaded M79 out in front of him more easily.

They climbed at a snail's pace, stopping every few feet to listen for unusual sounds. They listened particularly for the disconcerting quiet when jungle creatures stopped chirring, signaling the presence of predators, animal or man. Every time the deafening silence fell, John and Tan slithered into the heavier undergrowth to listen, then welcomed back the jungle's night song.

They moved quietly— one foot at a time— then stopped to listen and examine the jungle ahead after each few steps. Their pace was glacially slow, but they were combat alert, *sure* that there were VC on the island, detection an acute risk.

In stretches they were reduced to crawling on their bellies to get through tangled undergrowth. The heavy load of ordnance made them move awkwardly, and the branches and leaves of the jungle seemed to tug and pull on all parts of their gear, occasionally producing clumsy, unnatural noises they were sure the enemy would hear. Each noise made them wince, stop, listen, then wait to ride out the adrenaline surge that followed every encounter with the cloying palms and vines.

At 0200 hours, John and Tan thought they heard human voices and they froze in their tracks. Perhaps it was just a tropical bird calling in the night. Or was it?

As they neared the ridge below the summit a fat lizard scampered across their legs into the undergrowth. They held their breath to keep from laughing. They continued to crawl.

When they reached the ridge John said, "Tan, let's set our positions here below the hilltop. This is the perfect defensive position, just below the top of the ridge. It gives us field of fire on three sides, and a cliff forward— an impossible climb from the beach, and the best vantage point, even though we can't see as far up and down the coast. If we have to boogie, we can maneuver right along this ridge line to the cliff above our extraction point."

Tan said "Roger, Dai Uy. I can go to the top of the hill to scan the coast if you want."

"No, we need to stay together. If the VC are here and we're compromised, we'll have to leap-frog our way down the ridge to the cliff."

John and Tan settled themselves into a slight depression on the ridge, and prepared for contact from all sides. Tan set out Claymore mines in a 270 degree sector, all approaches covered.

When they were settled, John looked at his watch. 0330. It had taken them three and a half hours to navigate the jungle hill to their observation point. The post was not optimal: they could only see a 25 degree sector of the Cambodian coast. They had a good view of the small "hurricane hole" cove of the island's east side where gun runners would likely hide, but could not see the stretch of the cove's beach directly below the steep wooded ridge.

They spoke quietly, nervously for a while, established a watch and each remained alert through the night. As the night wore on, the wind picked up, rustled the brush around them, and made careful listening nearly impossible.

In the fifth hour both heard the undeniable sound of human voices speaking Vietnamese somewhere below them. John and Tan's first response was to prepare to engage. They determined the voices to be distant, then they strained to look over the ridge to the south edge of the cove where the voices seemed to originate. They could see nothing— no boats, no people.

John's watch read 0545, and dawn was nigh. He thought 'How did these guys sneak into the cove without us hearing them?'

John whispered, "Tan— load the M79 with HE and I'll position myself with the Winchester. We'll work east further out on the ridge, set up, wait for more light, and see how this plays out." Tan was already loading the M79 and strapping 40mm bandoliers across his chest.

They crawled quietly and invisibly east on the ridge to gain a vantage point to the south shore of the cove. No matter how far they moved, they could not see the VC below, but could just make out the sterns of two vessels.

'The audacity!' John thought. 'The VC sail slow moving barge-loads of ammo down the coast from Cambodia to resupply their troops in Vietnam. How could this go unnoticed until now?' He crept as far forward as he could to obtain the best sight angle and cradled the Winchester. Tan settled forward, 15 feet to John's left with the M79. Now, with just a little more light and the VC moving lazily about, they had every advantage.

Minutes seemed like hours till the sun finally broke the horizon and a fuzzy, orange light illuminated the cove. John signaled Tan to be alert. Tan was already gauging the target distance with the 79's ladder sight.

Suddenly, diesel engines erupted to life below them. Two barges appeared, edging slowly away from the beach with loincloth-clad Vietnamese on deck. John set his binoculars upon the largest deckhand. As the side of the barge slid into full sunlight, John was startled to see a bright red Pegasus painted on the hull, and that the big man was a Caucasian. He blew out his breath and nearly shouted to Tan—

"Fucking Mobilgas! American Oil company barges moving fuel up and down the coast. Check your fire!"

Tan laughed. "Close call, Dai Uy. We had them cold."

"Close indeed! Our Mobilgas friends have no idea how close." John wiped his hand over his face and shook his head. "Tan, how do we ever tell this story?"

They returned to their ridge post, cleared the Claymores, ate some LRRP lemon bars and awaited the 0700 extraction.

Ha Tien 1970

II. USS Tulsa (CLG-6)
1968

FREE FIRE ZONE

Medici wiped sleep from his eyes and caught his foot on the threshold of the watertight door to the pilot house. In his solar plexus he sensed tension among the watch standers.

"Navigator," he said to LCDR MacLeish. "It's 0745 and I'm ready to relieve you." When the ship stood port and starboard watches on the gun line, Medici relieved the Navigator, and he Medici, every six hours.

"Navigator! Do you have the exact coordinates of the free fire zone plotted yet?" boomed CAPT Burberry, TULSA's C/O. His mouth dropped off in a hook to one side.

"Yes, sir, Captain sir," stuttered MacLeish. The man had the worst case of nerves Medici had ever seen. The cigarette in his hand shook so violently it was almost a blur. His insecurity spread like poison gas, destroying the equanimity of those around him.

The Captain glared at MacLeish through the porthole to the bridge. On the chart in front of him MacLeish had plotted a wide rhomboid zone of red lines extending two miles seaward from the beach and emphasized its borders with red hash marks.

Medici read the legend on the lower right corner of the chart— "Vicinity of Danang, Republic of Viet Nam." They were back in I Corps, he surmised, just north of Danang. He looked out the portholes of the pilothouse through the Plexiglas windows of the bridge, and saw they were keeping station three miles off a white sand beach with way barely on. The beach contours matched the chart.

"Navigator, the free fire zone commences at 0800 Hotel according to the message from the Marine spotter, correct?"

"Aye-aye, sir. 0800 Hotel. Eleven minutes from now," MacLeish's

voice cracked.

"And you're sure of the coordinates?"

"Yes, sir. Triple-checked and plotted them. It's enclosed with the red hash marks on the chart."

"Ver' well," Burberry exhaled and turned to survey the beach with his binoculars. There wasn't a peep from anyone on the bridge.

Medici whispered to MacLeish, "I'm ready to relieve you, sir."

MacLeish looked at him with foggy cow eyes framed by unusually long lashes. For an instant Medici sensed the message 'You don't know what you're in for out here, kid,' before MacLeish briefed him on the tactical situation with no preliminaries.

The Marine naval gunfire spotters for the area had issued a message designating this beach a free fire zone for four hours this morning to coincide with South Korean Tiger Division operations just inland from the beach. The idea was that the Koreans' sweep would push North Vietnamese regulars to the beach where they could be cut down by naval gunfire since, once a free fire zone commenced, under the Rules of Engagement TULSA could shoot with abandon at anybody or anything that moved through it. The captain had pushed the ship through the night to reach the zone before 0800.

MacLeish pointed out the navigational landmarks, how the OOD had been maintaining position, the current's set and drift, the wind's speed and direction. "The old man's got a hard-on. There's blood in his eyes," MacLeish whispered to Medici. "Don't cross him today."

Medici nodded slowly, saluted. "I relieve you, sir."

"I stand relieved," the Navigator responded, then informed the bridge, "Mr. Medici has the navigation watch." He started to leave the bridge, then turned and said quietly to Medici, "Buzz me in the cabin if you have any problems," then left.

Burberry turned and glared through the porthole at Medici. "So we've got the Assistant Navigator with us now," he said in near falsetto. "What'd the Navigator need? Some tranquilizers?" He laughed. Ron Maint, Burberry's favorite OOD because he was a jock, laughed a little late.

"No, sir. Time to relieve the watch," Medici answered quietly.

54

"You sure you've got the tactical situation in hand, *Mister* Medici? We're going to be shooting soon."

Medici smarted at the Captain's sarcasm.

"I've got it, Captain." He glowered at Burberry.

"Good," Burberry said, taken aback by the insubordinate glare. He turned slowly toward the beach, still shaded by morning mist.

"It's 0800, Captain," cried the Bos'nmate of the Watch.

"Ver' well. Gun control, is Director Two awake?"

The Gun Control Officer spoke drawl into the mouthpiece of the sound powered phones: "Director Two, Gun Control. You 'wake, Johnny boy?" Control listened for a few seconds, then spoke out to the bridge. "They're up, alert and locked on the beach, Captain."

"Ver' well." Burberry scanned the beach with the big black tubes of the Zeiss 7x50s. Medici could almost smell the C/O's bloodlust. He knew Burberry was a son of a bitch, but he had not previously understood how naval gunfire was almost sexual for him. Medici had read that Burberry had been an officer on a submarine in World War II that had sunk more unarmed merchant tonnage than anyone in the Pacific. But that sub also had a whispered reputation for not picking up survivors, even thousands of miles from land in the South Pacific. Medici surmised the C/O of the sub liked doing it from a distance, like B-52 pilots. No mess, no blood, no screams, just black oily smoke.

Medici and his quartermasters carefully plotted a fix every five minutes on the large scale chart. The C/O wanted to know exactly where they were in relation to the red hash lines of the free fire zone. Precisely as Medici plotted the 0835 fix, a lookout yelled, "Large motor sampan to port, bearing 280 relative."

The watch standers ran to the port wing of the bridge. At once five pairs of binoculars flew to eye level. Medici saw a thirty-foot wooden sampan, laden with nets, baskets and eight passengers— men and women— moving north a mile off the beach. He took a bearing from the gyro-repeater, then asked Gun Control for a range from Director One's radar. He plotted the sampan on the chart with that information. The sampan was 800 yards outside the free fire zone heading slowly into it. It was so far off the beach, so slow, and the visibility from the ship so good that it could not have departed the beach from the zone without TULSA's crew observing it.

"Signal bridge, put the big eyes on it," Burberry shouted.

"Aye, sir, we have it. A thirty-foot motorized sampan. About eight zips aboard. See no weapons, just nets and bamboo poles...."

"Of course they show no weapons! They see a goddam cruiser bristling with barrels. They hide them under the nets and seats, just like the Japs used to on those merchantmen," Burberry yelled, excited now, a bit of spittle visible at the down turned corner of his mouth.

"Gun control, put the five-inch battery under local control of Director Two! Is Two locked on?" Burberry demanded.

Control spoke, then listened, then spoke again into the sound powered phones. "Captain, Two is locked on and has local control of the five-inch battery. But LT(jg) Aiken says there are women and children on the sampan. He can see them in his optics."

"Of course there're women and children. What better way to disguise their real purpose, transporting weapons! They're VC dammit, I know it!" His certainty made everyone on the bridge squirm. "Load and lock the five-inch battery. Tell Two to prepare to take them under fire."

Medici felt perspiration in his armpits and the small of his back as he spoke. "Captain!" he shouted, turning every head on the bridge. "They're not in the free fire zone." There was another hundred yards at best. All eyes turned to Medici, then to Burberry.

"Well, when *exactly* will they enter it, Assistant Navigator?" he shouted.

Medici leaned over the chart table, trying to stay calm, but his pencil hand shook. He calculated the sampan's speed, then added another 300 yards for possible zone boundary error, and said in a thick voice, "Four minutes, Captain. Cap'n, with their speed, distance from the beach and our range of visibility, they couldn't have left from the zone since we've been here...."

"*Mister* Medici," Burberry shouted, glaring at him, "when I want suppositions from a junior officer I'll ask for them. Tell me when the four minutes are up."

Medici felt as if he had interrupted a man in heat, ready to enter a woman. Nothing could stop Burberry now. Medici watched the black and white face of the 24-hour clock in front of him. The movement of the second hand seemed to drill and grind something within him. He wished he had the power to stop time. He couldn't. The 240 seconds passed— an eternity. He took one more bearing on the sampan, plotted it and said quietly, "They're in the free fire zone, Captain."

"Quartermaster, enter in ship's log that at 0847 Assistant Navigator LT(jg) Medici informed C/O that suspected enemy sampan had entered the free fire zone." Burberry grinned maniacally.

Medici couldn't believe the man's cowardice. The bloodlust was bad enough, but he had to pin the blame on someone else in case of an inquiry.

"Director Two, commence fire. Bracket and halve for range, then fire for effect," Burberry ordered.

Gun Control repeated the order into the sound powered phones, hesitated a second, then said, "Captain, LT(jg) Aiken says he clearly sees two children and three women in the sampan."

In a rage Burberry crossed to Gun Control and tore the sound powered phones from his head. He held the earphone to his ear and shouted, "LT(jg) Aiken, this is Captain Burberry. I have ordered you to commence fire on that sampan. Will you obey that order, or shall I relieve and court martial you?" He listened. "Very well, Mr. Aiken. Commence fire at will."

Before Gun Control had the phones back in place, the bridge clattered and their ears roared from the explosion erupting from the five-inch gun barrel barely five yards in front of them. No one had dropped the bridge windows or put in their earplugs yet. The enlisted watch scrambled to drop the Plexiglass panels as the second round boomed. Shredded wadding the color of cedar paper on good cigars drifted across the bridge deck like autumn leaves.

All eyes were on the sampan. It was so close to the ship, and the five inch's barrels depressed so far below level, that the first round hit 25 yards short. The big projectile skipped like a flat rock off the surface of the water, flew over the sampan and detonated on the white sand beach. The sampan passengers gazed at the ship. The second round landed just short of the sampan and detonated in a huge gray geyser. The concussion heeled the boat and spilled its passengers into the South China Sea.

"Captain, Director Two wants to know if he should cease fire," Gun Control said.

"God dammit, Charlie, I'll tell him when I want to cease fire. Tell them to load AP rounds."

"Excuse me, Captain. Anti-personnel rounds have distance-altitude fuses. We're too close to target. They won't detonate. Neither will white phosphorous," Gun Control explained reluctantly.

"Ver' well. Then continue with high explosive, but resume goddam fire."

The fifth round hit the wooden hull squarely, sending splintered planks and bamboo poles in all directions in what appeared to Medici to be slow motion. He could see heads bobbing in the water. A forearm that had held onto the hull was blown off and tumbled like a large white stick thrown for a dog to fetch. The sixth round slapped off the water like the first, skimmed to the beach, skidded up the sand and destroyed a large palm tree. The trunk fell gracefully out of the tree line, spilling green coconuts as it crashed to the white sand.

"Captain, the Koreans are just beyond the beach. These long rounds are a hazard to them," Gun Control entreated.

"Okay, Charlie, cease fire. I'm going to my sea cabin. Mr. Maint, you have the conn and the deck."

Burberry left the bridge. Medici formed a mental picture of him masturbating away his blood lust in the tiny cabin. Then, as Burberry reached the door, the ship's doctor, Harry Bennett, approached and entered the sea cabin with him. After ten minutes the doc came to the bridge. The OOD's phone from the Captain's cabin buzzed and Maint answered. He said, "Aye, aye, sir," and cradled it, then announced, "We're going alongside to pick up survivors. All ahead one-third. Steer 278. Man the port motor whaleboat." He looked confused to Medici, despite the crisp commands.

Medici was boat officer. He couldn't be two places at once, so he buzzed the Navigator who came to the bridge sleepily to relieve him while he handled the boat detail.

The ship crawled alongside the hulk 10 minutes later. The ship's old Bos'n had rigged the accommodation ladder so men could bring survivors aboard. They were so close the whaleboat was unnecessary. Swimmers brought in the survivors.

Three gray-haired Vietnamese males wept impassively, one without a left forearm, save a bloody stump. One held his hand up and kept saying, "No VC. No VC." Two women and one child were peppered with high explosive shrapnel. The other child had a wide bamboo splinter through his groin and out his buttock. The third woman wailed uncontrollably, clutching the children.

The splintered hull lay awash, nets floating in a large circle filled with wicker baskets, dead fish and bloody water. Sailors found no guns or ammunition in the wreck. Medici looked up from his whaleboat and caught a glimpse of John Aiken, still on watch in Director Two, staring down at the carnage, looking as if he had just lost his best friend.

Dr. Bennett treated the wounded with battle dressings and tourniquets on the main deck, port side. Blood and lymph and feces stained the cruiser's teak planking. The prissy X/O came down to the main deck.

"Harry, did you find evidence confirming that they were VC?" he asked.

"No, X/O, just these proper Republic of Vietnam civilian ID cards." The doctor proffered the thick stack of ID cards and identity papers to the X/O.

The X/O scowled, snatched the cards from the doctor, and said "You know these cards are easily forged by VC to cover their smuggling operations!" He turned smartly and left to collect the film from cameras any sailors had used to film the incident.

A MEDEVAC helo arrived and the survivors were carried to the fantail for transfer to the hospital ship in Danang. The X/O had not permitted the survivors to be brought into the ship's sick bay from the main deck, as if they were lepers. In a way they were, Medici thought, infected victims of the C/O's moral contagion.

The crew hosed the deck with seawater, then holystoned it to remove the stains. Some of the bloodstains would not come off.

In the afternoon Burberry spoke to the ship's company on the 1 MC to tell them that as a result of the day's action and confirmed VC WIAs, the Marine spotter unit was putting TULSA in for a citation. He concluded, "I'm proud as punch of TULSA's officers and men." Medici spit into his stateroom sink.

Just before dinner Medici encountered John Aiken as he stood in the doorway of his tiny stateroom. John, an Annapolis graduate, loomed tall and thin in the haze gray doorframe. Normally he spoke with a southerner's soft speech. Now he spoke jerkily and had the worst hangdog look Medici had ever seen, like a guilty basset hound. Aiken held a Navy form in his hand.

"Jesus, John, what did it feel like?" Medici asked excitedly. "We've never shot so close before."

"Huh, well... I don't know. It was just shooting." He paused. "I didn't want to do it, Tom. When the Captain got on the sound powered phones and threatened to relieve me I saw Annapolis and my graduation flash in front of my eyes."

Aiken raised his eyes to Medici. "I felt I had to follow his direct orders, even though I saw those women and kids...." He spoke the last words slowly, his gaze beyond Medici, back to the scene of the morning's carnage. After a moment he focused back on Medici. "I was wrong. I should have made him relieve me."

"Don't say that, John. I thought about it too. If I'd been in the director I would have fired in a hot second, despite what we saw. At least I think I would," Medici said. He tried to imagine shooting the innocents, on some primitive level even enjoying the carnage. But immediately a wave of nausea traveled through him at the thought. Then he thought of the tens of thousands of rounds Tulsa had fired under spotters' directions, and wondered what the actual results were, because the ship never saw first hand.

Aiken looked at him without comprehension, then with the understanding of one who has been there for one who hasn't. He looked down at the form he held.

"Well, all I know is, I put in my papers with the X/O for transfer to Naval Supply School today. No more of this Surface Line officer shit for me. I'll push papers for the rest of my four years." He chuckled, took a step away from the door, then lay down on his bunk facing the bulkhead. He said nothing more.

Medici walked slowly down the passageway wondering if he did the right thing signing up for the Navy, but the thought left him before he reached the wardroom.

Vinh Lang Co RVN 1968

SETTING THE HOOK

"You mean they really have jobs like this in the navy?" Medici asked Andrew Guleen of the Rand Corporation after his speech to Medici's Vietnamese language class at the Naval Amphibious Base in Coronado.

Guleen smiled at Medici's awe: He had hooked another NILO, he was sure.

"Of course they do. Do you expect Admiral Zumwalt and Captain Rectanus to rely on intelligence from the Army and CIA?" He laughed. "We've got forty thousand men in country— the least we can do for our sailors is have our own active intelligence apparatus. Captain Rectanus is a smart man, legendary in intelligence circles. It was his idea to hand pick young officers, promote them to full Lieutenant and put them in the field on independent duty running agent networks. A brilliant if unorthodox stroke that has paid dividends for naval intelligence."

He put his pipe back in his mouth, drew on it for scholarly effect, and let the hook sink deeper in Medici's imagination.

He had this identical conversation several times before, and each time it worked. If anything, Guleen had become more subtle in playing the potential NILO volunteer. Usually they were gung-ho NROTC grads, but he had found the Ivy Leaguers increasingly receptive, due to their sense of *noblesse oblige* and Hemingway idolatry. Good qualities to troll for, to Shanghai— no, "head hunt"— young naval officers to run the navy's special spy networks in Indochina. The combination was irresistible: exotic independent duty, spy ambiance, spot promotion to full Lieutenant, flight and combat pay. Just about the best package the navy had to offer a junior officer for a one-year tour of duty. And you never could tell who'd bite, Guleen thought, watching Medici scratch his head and read the NILO job description.

Coronado, CA 1969

A SIGNAL FROM THE ADMIRAL

"Guthrie, go down to the Chief's Mess and get me a real coffee mug, not this candy-ass thing from the wardroom," Medici said as he threw the empty crockery coffee cup through the porthole between the bridge and the pilothouse.

Guthrie bobbled, then caught the mug and laughed, "Aye, aye, sir!" and sent the messenger of the watch to fetch it. The enlisted watchstanders liked even this 4-to-8 a.m. stint when LT(jg) Medici was OOD. He was irreverent, fair, and a good shipdriver. Besides, they were on their way to Hawaii for a two-week visit. The duty aboard a stateside flagship was pure heaven compared to the two years they had done as Seventh Fleet Flagship in Vietnam and the western Pacific during the height of the war.

"OD, it won't be like this when we get to Hawaii. No mid-watches. No steaming. Just hula girls, mai tais and pineapples," Guthrie said, reflecting the sentiments of the watch crew.

"Didn't I tell you Second Division deck apes have been chosen to paint out the ship while we're in Hono, Guthrie?" Medici said to the mock groans of the watch.

"Mr. Medici, is it too late to put in a leave chit for our two weeks in Hawaii?" Guthrie responded quickly. As Leading Petty Officer of Second Division, Medici was his Division Officer.

"Maybe we'll paint her back in San Diego instead," Medici mused, then peered into the hooded radar screen. "Where's the goddam E.T.? This Pathfinder is still down and we're into the Molokai Pass," Medici said. "Is that you Ferrante, you meatball? Why can't you fix this thing?" Medici said and shined his red beam toward the figure lumbering toward him from the darkened wing of the bridge.

"Admiral's on the bridge!" Guthrie shouted.

Oh shit, Medici thought. "Good morning, Admiral," he said, delivering a smart salute in the dark.

"Good morning, Lieutenant. Radar's still down I gather?"

"Yes, Admiral, but we should have daylight in a few minutes."

Rear Admiral Harms, the Reserve Chief of Naval Intelligence, a guest of First Fleet Commander on this cruise, hoisted his ample bulk into the red leather C/O's and fleet commander's chair at the starboard corner of the bridge. Harms, an early riser, had attended the 4-to-8 watch each day, and occupied the chair. It was the first time any of them including Medici had seen someone other than the fleet's admiral in the seat. But the watch was flattered to have a real live admiral there to keep them company. It kept them all on their toes, as they tried to demonstrate to him the snappy flagship seamanship of which they were all proud.

"You know, Lieutenant, I've always enjoyed the 4-to-8. It gives a man time to organize his thoughts before the day's round begins. It's quite an insight to nature to watch the sea changes through sunrise." The admiral peered through the bridge windows, sweeping the horizon with his gaze. "Looks pretty quiet this morning."

"We passed a couple of small inter-island freighters close aboard just as I relieved the watch, but we're full into the Molokai Pass now. I'm concerned about head-on traffic with our small boat radar down. No one's going to overtake us at 22 knots. We've entered the submarine lanes though," Medici added.

After a moment the admiral said, "I thought we might chat a little more about your experience with our detailers in Washington. I've been a reserve officer most of my career, and I don't much like it when a reserve gets jerked around because he's not regular navy."

"Certainly, Admiral, but there's not much more to tell. Excuse me a minute," Medici said as he walked toward the voice tube at center bridge. A few feet on the other side stood his JOOD, picking his face. "Mr. Bost, are you ready to take the conn?"

Bost shot up straight, "Yuh, yes, sir!"

"Then assume the conn," Medici said patiently.

Bost poked his head through the port to the wheel house, "This is

Mr. Bost and I have the conn," he said, in a wavering voice.

"Aye, aye, sir," came the chorus from the bridge watch.

"This is Mr. Medici, Mr. Bost has the conn and I have the deck."

Again the chorus sang, "Aye, aye, sir." Medici walked back to the admiral's chair, stood next to the left armrest and continued to scan the horizon as he spoke.

"I flew to Washington from San Diego at my own expense when that message came out saying all junior officers would be transferred to different commands for the second eighteen months of their tours. I had applied to Naval Intelligence from OCS since I had written a thesis at Princeton analyzing Voice of America as a propaganda instrument. It got me honors. Back then the detailer told me that only regular navy got those jobs, but that if I put in my first tour at sea, they would transfer me into intelligence for my second.

"Well, when we found out that everybody on the flagship would be transferred to slow moving LSTs delivering toilet paper to Vietnam from Guam, that was it. So I went to Washington to talk with my line detailer about the second tour with Naval Intelligence, as I felt it had been held out to me. He laughed and told me that we all have to do our duty, that the Navy had responsibilities in Vietnam and that he had no jurisdiction over intelligence billets. I looked at his ribbons and he'd never been to Nam and I'd already been there a year, so I asked him, 'When are you going, Lieutenant?'"

The admiral bellowed a laugh.

"That ended our conversation. Except he told me rather frigidly that I could go talk to the intelligence detailer, which I did. Same story, flip side. The intelligence detailer would like to have me, but he has no jurisdiction over line officers. Hence my description of the process as 'ping-pong'. I think the detailers are screwing the reserve officers."

Medici walked over to the gyro-repeater to check their course heading. They were steaming 4 degrees to starboard of their plotted course. "Mind your helm, Mr. Bost." Bost gave the same conning command to the quartermaster at the helm. It permitted him to steer back on course as he saw fit. Medici returned to the admiral's chair.

"I hope your conclusion is incorrect," said Harms, staring at the relative wind indicators above his head. First light could just be seen on the horizon off the port quarter. The sea ahead changed from black to leaden gray. "But I've heard similar stories from other reserve officers. This Vietnam episode has provided some nasty divisions within the service. I'm afraid the core career officers don't believe in it or support it. They think all the men entering the navy now do so simply to avoid the draft. Hence, they assign new reserves to the less career-oriented, and frankly more dangerous billets. Meanwhile, they stay fat and happy in choice traditional billets where they won't get shot. I'm afraid so far the regular navy doesn't look at Vietnam as career enhancing, mostly just duty to be avoided by career officers."

"It doesn't surprise me, Admiral. It's just disappointing," Medici said, automatically scanning the sea ahead of them. "It's not a real incentive to stay— MEDICI— I HAVE CONN— LEFT FULL RUDDER!" he bellowed, running to the gyro-repeater and pushing Bost out of the way. Through the transit on the repeater he tracked the black hull of a nuclear submarine 1500 yards ahead, hoping it would pass cleanly down the starboard side. The ship heeled heavily to starboard as the rudder was put over. Within seconds the submarine had also altered course to port to freeze the narrowing distance between them. The sub was traveling close to 17 knots, the relative speed between them 45 mph head on, a supersonic closing speed for surface vessels. Medici perspired freely in the damp air, his nerve endings letting go, allowing the free circulation of animal flight. His heart pounded audibly.

"Damn. He wasn't showing his Grimes light," Medici said. The flashing yellow beacon would have enabled them to see the sub a mile further away even in the confused sea and gray dawn.

He pushed the talk button on the intercom to the signal bridge. "Signalman. Signal 'Good morning from USS TULSA' to the sub by light."

"Aye, aye, sir," came from the tinny speaker.

The sub responded, "Sorry about that. Good morning and safe voyage," without identifying herself. The nuclear subs wore no hull numbers and never identified themselves, so critical was the security of their positions in the nuclear deterrent game. When the sub was clear past, Medici returned to course and said, "Sorry, Admiral. Great recommendation of my ship driving abilities! Mr. Bost, please resume the conn."

"I didn't see her either, even after you started your turn, nor did the lookouts. I'm glad you caught her." Then he raised his voice so all could hear, "As Thucydides correctly said two thousand years ago, 'A collision at sea can ruin your whole day!'" The bridge watch laughed. The admiral's remark defused the tension. Full dawn had broken. Visibility ahead was three miles. Bost scanned ahead with the 7x50 binoculars as if there was sex in it for him.

The admiral continued in a lower voice.

"I appreciate your conclusion about the treatment you've gotten from the detailers. It happens that the Chief of Naval Personnel was my roommate at Annapolis. I shall send a signal to him today through flag channels. I expect we'll get some results shortly. My compliments to your captain." He hefted himself out of the chair and left the bridge.

Medici loved it when this admiral spoke of "sending signals." It was the purely anachronistic navy jargon Horatio Hornblower used in C. S. Forester's novels to describe flag hoist communication. It gave Medici a comfortable feeling of the tradition and continuity of the naval service.

The two-week stay in Hawaii was uneventful and boring, except for the visit of Admiral Hyland, Commander in Chief Pacific Fleet. He had served aboard Tulsa as Commander Seventh Fleet, and felt great nostalgia for the ship and its crew. Medici happened to have the in-port deck watch when Hyland, a balding man with twinkling eyes, came aboard. He met, chatted and joked with him for several minutes before the official party went below. Rumor had it that Hyland might be elevated to Chief of Naval Operations. It was a small navy, and you never knew when the contact and same-ship camaraderie would help.

Tulsa's new C/O, Ed Hanford, had become Medici's mentor. Hanford was the best C/O and ship driver Medici had seen. They quickly grew to respect each other and Medici was the only officer not a department head allowed direct access to the captain at any time. Their relationship had cemented in Sydney on their trip home to the States when Medici spent 26 hours a day coordinating the ship's machine shops in order to repair the American sailing yacht *Orion II* in time for the start of the Sydney-Hobart race on Boxing Day, Dec. 26. The yacht had been dismasted by a white squall in the Indian Ocean on her way to Sydney for the race. The owner, Huey Short, had been Hanford's classmate at Annapolis for a year, and they had known each other during the captain's attaché tour in Buenos Aires. It became a matter of national pride to render *Orion* shipshape and seaworthy.

A new mast from Hamburg was air freighted by German Freres, and TULSA's machine shop worked night and day to machine clevis pins and fittings for her standing rigging. She was rigged and tuned by nightfall on Christmas Day, and the ship's company listened daily to Australian short wave radio to see how *Orion* was doing in the long and dangerous race. She won, to the pride of the crew and especially Hanford and Medici.

After that, besides observing Medici's ship driving, Hanford scrutinized him carefully. Then, shortly after they returned to San Diego, he confided to Medici that he was being reviewed by the flag officer selection board for Rear Admiral, an early promotion, and that he wanted Medici to be his flag lieutenant. Medici was quietly excited until Hanford wasn't selected first time around, and the naval detailers informed all reserve junior officers that they would be transferred to Vietnam tours for their second 18 months.

It was at that point Medici traveled to Washington for the disappointing talks with the detailers. He was an enthusiastic junior officer looking to avoid a terminally dull existence on a LST anchored off Vietnam, or carrying toilet paper from Guam.

On the cruise back from Hawaii they engaged in underway refueling with the USS MISPILLION, an oiler. Shot lines, hawsers, wire cables and fuel hoses were brought over, and Hanford let Medici keep station from the starboard wing of the open bridge. An UNREP— underway replenishment— required station keeping within 110 to 120 feet of the oiler at her exact speed of 12 knots, a matter of some finesse. Rudder orders were not given by angle such as "Left standard rudder," but by quarters of degrees, "Steer 083 and 1/4" or "Steer 083 and 1/2;" engine speed orders were spoken "Indicate 124 revolutions" instead of "All ahead standard." The increments were smaller than could actually be steered or controlled, but conveyed to the helmsman and engineman the nuances of direction and speed necessary to keep station accurately.

The C/O of the MISPILLION was a comedian. The oiler had just returned from a tour in the Tonkin Gulf off Vietnam. He solicited the donation of a huge UNION 76 orange globe from the oil company in California, and at his expense, mounted the six-foot ball high on the second deck astern. Combatant ships came alongside the tanker in the Tonkin Gulf for night refueling. At the moment the fuel hose was hooked and ready to pump, the MISPILLION's C/O would switch on the light in the orange 76 globe as if a stateside filling station, and ask the OOD on the telephone line, "Fill her up?" Lore had it that sometimes the oiler would send two men over on a highline with squirt bottles and squeegees. Landing on deck, they would run to the bridge and wash all the windows, then ask the C/O, "Can we check the oil in the main reduction gears for you today, Captain?" Finally, near the end of refueling, before they returned to the oiler, the station attendants would produce a Union Oil credit charge slip, and write it up for perhaps 130,000 gallons of Naval Service Fuel Oil at 50 cents/gallon for a total of $65,000. In the license box they would put the ship's official naval hull number, then say, "That's okay, we'll put it on your tab," if the C/O said he hadn't a Union Oil card. It was the best gag on Yankee Station. The boost to morale of the crews on both ships was incalculable. TULSA's crew laughed all evening.

The refueling lasted through dinner hour. By the time the 1 MC announced "All secured" and the ship went back to steaming routine, it was 9 P.M. Medici just made it to the tail end of the late sitting in the wardroom. He chose a seat next to an unassuming commander with three new gold stripes on the shoulder boards of his tropical whites, a member of the First Fleet Staff. Medici introduced himself and sat down.

"Good evening, I'm Tom Medici, ship's company."

"Hi, I'm Ron Hamm, Chief of Staff for air ops. Got the refueling detail finished?"

"Yes, sir. It was my first as an OOD."

"Please call me Ron. Congratulations. You did a fine job from what I saw. 'Course I don't know if that's a compliment from a navy pilot!" They both laughed, then ate for awhile.

"Ron, I don't know why but your name is very familiar. I'm sure we haven't met before," Medici said between bites.

Hamm chuckled. "You might have seen it in *Stars and Stripes,* the military rag."

Medici dropped his fork with a clank, incredulous.

"You mean you're the guy of Hanoi fame? 'Happy' Hamm?"

"I don't know if fame is the right word," he said soberly.

"You single-handedly took out Hanoi's power plant in a thunderstorm, at night, in an A-6, if I remember correctly," Medici gaped.

"I didn't have much choice. We were eleven miles from Hanoi when I lost my wingman. It was just as dangerous on the route out and you don't want to be hit carrying six 1000-lb. bombs, so we thought what the hell, might as well go in and dump the eggs."

"But in a thunderstorm? It said you knocked the huge rotor right off its mounts. It was inoperative for months."

"You've got a good memory. That was a lucky shot. You can never hope to place them that well, even from an A-6 that flies on terrain radar. To it, rain and darkness are not even complications." He paused and sipped some milk. "Actually, my navigator should get most of the credit. He did an outstanding job."

Medici's eyes dropped to Hamm's chest. He hadn't recognized the first award, a dark blue ribbon with a vertical gold stripe. It was the Navy Distinguished Service Medal— 3 awards, then the Silver Star— 3 awards, and the Distinguished Flying Cross— 3 awards.

"That's three Navy DSMs, three Silver Stars and three DFCs, right? All in one war?"

"Yes. But a lot of other guys deserved them in my squadron." The whole matter obviously embarrassed Hamm so Medici dropped the subject. The wardroom seemed singularly quiet during the lapse. Only the two of them were still at table.

The pantry door flew open with an annoying metallic crash and a white-coated steward, Corazon, came in with a handful of letters.

"Combander 'Amm, you got somb lettuhs at de mail call. They had mail for us on de oiler. You too, Mr. Medici." He gave Medici two letters, both official looking.

Medici opened the first. The envelope showed "Flag Quarters, St. Michaels, Md" as return address. Stationery inside bore a blue flag with three white stars in triangular pattern. Below it appeared the legend "The Chief of Naval Personnel." It was a letter from CNP to Admiral Harms who had stood bridge watches with Medici:

> "Dear Bob,
>
> This is in reply to your message concerning Lieutenant (junior grade) Thomas Medici, Jr., USNR.
>
> I share your concern for this young officer but let me assure you that he is not a ping-pong ball between two detailers. In a personal visit to the Bureau in May he again reiterated his desire for an intelligence billet for his next assignment. He was told that while his college background made him a good candidate for such an assignment, there were few available for an officer of his seniority. He was also told that our highest priority requirements for junior officers were at sea or in Vietnam.
>
> Since his visit we have screened him and plan to detach him from TULSA in September to commence training on 6 October for ultimate assignment to the Intelligence Division of the Staff of Commander Naval Forces Vietnam. This will greatly enhance his opportunity for his change of designator in his final year of service which in any case is any time after February 1970.
>
> I appreciate your interest in this fine young officer, and hope that we will be able to retain him.

Sincerely,
Charles K. Duncan
Vice Admiral USN"

The letter was signed "Charley" with the additional note "Glad to see you at the flag officers conference."

At the bottom in a shaky ballpoint script was a note from RADM Harms to Medici: "I hope this will be of interest. Told you I would get some sort of action.

Best regards,
Bob Harms"

The second official letter was from the fat smug line detailer in Washington, indicating Medici would shortly be detached for training and assignment to the Intelligence Staff of Commander Naval Forces Vietnam.

Where was the staff located, Medici wondered. In Saigon, or the field somewhere with the riverboats and firefights going on all around? Frankly, he had in mind duty as Naval Attaché in London or Paris, not Vietnam. This was ridiculous. He had just finished a year in the combat zone on TULSA and now would be going back for a second tour when guys like the fat detailer had never gone. And how about his wife? He wasn't sure the marriage could stand a year's separation right now.

Then he thought, dammit it's not fair. As soon as they got back to San Diego he would call the Congressman he had worked for one summer, a family friend and powerful member of the House Rules Committee, about getting the orders changed. Hadn't his cousin Philip been pulled out of his army unit and sent to Germany, when all others had been sent to Vietnam?

"Something wrong?" Ron Hamm asked.

"No. Just got some personal news. I guess I'm not so hungry. Will you excuse me?" He got up and left the wardroom with the letters partially crushed in his perspiring hand.

Medici drafted a letter to Congressman O'Brien the day before the ship returned to San Diego and posted it in the ship's mail. In essence it said, "I've already spent a year in the combat zone. Why do I have to go again? Can you do anything about it?"

When TULSA came alongside the mole pier at North Island, San Diego, his wife was waiting in their yellow Cougar with black vinyl roof, a present from her parents when she graduated from Wellesley. She came aboard but he left her in the wardroom with the other animated, chatting officers' wives, the electricity of imminent sexual intercourse heavy in the air. He secured his division spaces, made sure all the boats were up and running, and rechecked the watchbill— any busywork not to have to tell her yet about the orders to Vietnam.

The wardroom crowd dwindled. He returned and suggested they leave. She gave him that pissy "I'm miffed because you've been ignoring me" look, then smiled at the new blond surfer-ensign who had the deck watch.

The Cougar was parked at the edge of the pier aimed straight across the bay at the Kona Kai Club on Shelter Island. Medici got behind the wheel and laughed.

"We lost steering control on the day we left for Hawaii and steamed directly toward the Kona Kai. You should have seen the expression on the faces of the people eating lunch there!" He laughed again. She didn't.

"Nonie, remember the admiral I told you about who stood 4-to-8 watches with me? Well the sonofabitch was the reserve Chief of Naval Intelligence. And you know what? He got me orders to an intelligence billet instead of LSTs in Guam!" No response. She looked straight ahead over the bay. "That's the good news. The bad news is it's in Vietnam."

She continued to look straight ahead, didn't even flinch. "Kathy Cernan let it slip in the wardroom," she said flatly. "That's a year's unaccompanied tour. What do you expect me to do?" she said coldly.

"Well, the job's actually at Naval Headquarters Staff, probably in Saigon. Maybe you could come over and live there. I've heard of wives doing that...."

"Right, I go there and sit around some sleazy apartment 12

hours a day while you do your spook stuff, then can't even talk to me about it. I don't speak a word of Vietnamese. Sounds great."

"Well, look, I'm not real pleased either. I sent a letter to Congressman O'Brien to see if he could get the orders changed. Of course, the change might be to LSTs at Guam. I'm not sure which is worse." The fact hit him that, either way, they probably would be separated for a year. In WESTPAC he had seen her a total of 39 days in 10 months. His eyes misted. He looked straight out over the bay.

"You're not sure what's worse!" She tensed her frame. "You and your damn NAVY!" She turned away and stared out the passenger window.

He started the car and headed through Coronado, down the strand to Imperial Beach. Off to the left they watched the Coronado Ferry plying to the Broadway Pier in San Diego. The skyline was crisp blue, interrupted only by the great gray stanchions and red steel sections of the uncompleted Coronado Bridge.

For some reason Nonie's remark about his damn navy superseded the problem of the orders to Vietnam. He found himself re-thinking his whole attitude. He had signed up as a volunteer to cast his lot with those who served during Vietnam, not the wanglers and evaders who went to the national guard or graduate school, or who ran to Canada or married and had children for a deferment. And now, he was caught between a rock and a hard place; the orders and his wife's attitude. It cleared the smoke in his head.

Next day on TULSA, after quarters, he used the ship's autovon line to telephone O'Brien in Washington. The ancient administrative aid, Miss Hicks, gushed over his call and said they had reviewed his letter and would call in chips at the Pentagon to try to get the orders changed. O'Brien came on the line for the last part of her explanation. He greeted Medici in his gruff style.

"How the hell are you, Lieutenant? You keeping those goddamn Viet Cong under control?" he bellowed.

"Well, that's why I called, Mr. O'Brien. I hope I haven't put you and Miss Hicks to too much trouble already, but I'm going to accept the orders to Vietnam. A lot of other guys have gone, and there's no reason I should get special treatment. Please just ignore my letter. I'm going." The silence from their end was deafening. "I've got some leave coming. Maybe I can come by and see you all in DC before I start language school."

"Sure, Tom, we'd be glad to see you. Maybe you should do the White House tour and some of the things you missed when you worked here...." O'Brien stopped himself short when he realized the implication of his suggestion.

"We'll see how much time I can get. Thanks again for the consideration. See you soon." He hung up.

Medici felt elated all day. A huge unspeakable burden was off his shoulders. He told his wife calmly at dinner. She said nothing, showed no expression, just got up and left the table, her dinner only half eaten.

That night Medici had a vivid dream that unsettled him for days afterward. He was dressed in blotchy camouflage fatigues which smelled a week old, and he had a week's growth of beard. He was lying crooked on a hillside in Laos or Cambodia in the shade of some strange evergreens which covered the slope. He was nestled up to his neck in the fallen needles. The hillside looked down into a valley which stood in bright sunlight. Ten thousand North Vietnamese regulars proceeded free-step through the valley. He saw their gray uniforms with the inscription "Born in the North, Die in the South" and their gray-brown pith helmets. They all wore gray, high-top canvas combat sneakers. Each carried a Russian AK-47 assault rifle with two banana clips and a single bandolier of cartridges. Diagonally across each back was a tubular canvas sock filled with short-grained rice. None smiled or even chatted. Only the muffled *ddrrrummppp* of 20,000 canvas shoes could be heard over the murmur of the wind in the pines. He awoke perspiring heavily. He hadn't made a sound during the dream, unconsciously afraid that the NVA would hear the sound, capture and torture him. His wife was still asleep, face turned away from him, as far over on her side of the bed as she could lie.

He got up quietly and drank a quart of water. His hand was

shaking as he held the glass. He wondered what he would do if the dream were a reality. Other than remaining absolutely still, he could think of nothing. A single weapon would be utterly useless confronted with those odds. He went to the bookcase and pulled André Malraux's novel of Cambodia *The Royal Way* from the shelf and re-read most of it before he fell asleep in his reading chair.

Next morning his wife found him there and told him to get ready quickly in order to make 7am quarters on TULSA. He pulled on a working khaki uniform, but waited to shave on the ship. They spoke ten words between them on the drive up the strand to Coronado. Things were not going well, Medici concluded.

After quarters someone on First Fleet Staff told him not to worry, Naval Forces Vietnam Staff was in fact in Saigon and like all other staffs— rear echelon. None went to combat; they just shuffled papers. His worst problem would be what bars to hang out in and what whores to choose. Medici didn't find this funny, but felt some relief about the staff job— at least he wasn't going to be a grunt. He got the FPO address for the Staff in Saigon and wrote a letter to the Admiral's Chief of Staff in keeping with good navy ettiquette on being assigned to a new command:

"Dear Captain Rainerd,

I am currently a LT(jg) on USS TULSA, the First Fleet Flagship. We have recently returned from WESTPAC where we were deployed as 7th Fleet flagship for 2 years. I was an OODI, Asst. Navigator, 2d Div Officer and Boat Officer.

I have recently been ordered in to N-2 Div of COMNAVFORV Staff, to report Dec. 3, 1969.

On TULSA, with embarked staff, we were required to deal with formalities and protocol of visits by international dignitaries. I presume some of the same occurs in Saigon. Is it necessary to bring dress white uniforms, medals, sword, etc. for COMNAVFORV duty?

Is there anything else in particular it is recommended to

bring? I would appreciate any information you could supply in this regard.

Yours truly,
Thomas N. Medici
LT(jg) USNR
USS TULSA CLG-6

Within two weeks he received a reply. A Xerox copy of his letter with the handwritten scrawl, "Tell LT(jg) Medici to bring his sword so he can cut crumpets at tea time each day at four. Tell him to make out a will. –C.O.S." Attached was a mimeographed letter from some lieutenant telling the newly ordered staff officer to bring plenty of wash and wear Khakis— fatigues and weapons would be supplied as needed in Saigon.

The Chief of Staff's's note stung Medici. If this was the attitude of the staff, it could be a long, shitty year. 'Wait and see,' he told himself.

The following weeks passed quickly. He detached at the end of August and returned to the ship just after Labor Day weekend to discover that Capt. Hanford had been taken to Balboa Naval Hospital after one of his migraines became a seizure. He was undergoing tests for a possible tumor. Medici and his wife were leaving the next day for their 30-day trip around the country. He vowed to visit the captain before he started Vietnamese language and survival schools when they returned.

Their trip around the country had the tinge of last rites. They visited all her relatives, except her uncle who was hunting big game on safari. Her aunt entertained them tepidly at her Lake Forest home. Medici came from a family of judges and lawyers. He increasingly got the feeling that Nonie was not concerned with duty or accomplishment. He hoped he was wrong.

They returned to San Diego and he began Vietnamese language school.

San Diego 1969

FROG LOVE

I remember Medici from Vietnamese language school at Coronado. We were all jaygees then. Most of us had come off other ships or shore commands and were training for a year in-country.

He was a little weird, even then. He did very well with the language; he seemed to have an ear for it. Our little bitty Vietnamese instructor, Ba Hoan, had been high falutin' in Saigon. Her husband had been the Minister of Agriculture and she was a teacher in a French Catholic lycee. Anyway, they left to come to the U.S. and now she was teaching language to naval officers and he was starting a restaurant, just so's they don't have to go back.

My point is she's got this real high tone about her and a lot of dignity about her country and its culture and its beauty, and all the time us poor dicks are scared shit about getting shot or blown up or whatever. The vocabulary is all about rocket launchers, tanks, machine guns, grenades, ambushes, and frogmen.

Near the end of the course Ba Hoan started giving us essay assignments. We were to use the vocabulary to date and any other we had learned on our own. Medici had of course gone over to San Diego State and bought his own Vietnamese-English dictionary— he always had to know more than anyone else about what we were studying— and used it to prepare his last essay. Ba Hoan said we should try to do something more imaginative than "I got ambushed— Call in artillery— We need medic immediately—" kind of stuff. Medici said that it was hard to do with the limited weaponry vocabulary, but he would try.

Next day he comes in with this two-page essay in Vietnamese— like a children's story really— that starts off about a navy frogman assigned to examine hulls of ships in the Saigon river for limpet mines. He describes basically boring duty until one day he glimpses what he thinks is a frog woman swimming around one of the ships and is immediately taken with her. He can't quite catch her, but sees her again on several occasions, lays a frog-trap and snares her. She is literally a "frog-woman" with whom he falls in love and they live under the piers in Saigon raising frog babies.

It's hard to describe the effect of the story on the class. We thought Medici was cracking up before he was even sent over, but then remembered he had already been there a year on his ship. Ba Hoan thought it was cute, but she was a little nervous that Medici was either spoofing her, making fun of her country's language, or cracking up. Medici just sat there with this shit-eating grin on his face after he read it, looking at each of us, then Ba Hoan, until everybody started to chuckle a little then laugh.

What he made us realize was how deeply scared and self-indulgent we all were worrying about learning enough of this really strange language to call in fire support or get a Vietnamese medic to stop the bleeding.

His silly frog-love story made us see it was unlikely any of what we learned was going to save our lives, that simply going to Vietnam and the vagaries of war was what would endanger our lives, so why not lie back and enjoy it with a bit of spoofing?

Tension that had been building in the class was released that day. Now that I think about it, it was a good thing, but at the time it seemed really weird. Know what I mean?

Coronado, CA 1969

Before...

III. Princeton and Washington 1966-67

LAUNDROMAT

At 6:15 a.m. each morning, after showering and putting on a clean oxford shirt and tie, Medici would drive his old Nash Rambler without air conditioning down Connecticut Avenue to the new Rayburn House Office Building where his Member of Congress— Jim O'Brien from the "Archie Bunker" Ninth District of Queens, New York— had his palatial congressional office. By the time he got to the underground parking his shirt was soaking wet from the heat and humidity.

As second ranking member of Rules Committee behind Tip O'Neill, O'Brien had his choice of suites in the brand new, highly air conditioned building. Medici arrived early to enter the cafeteria as it opened at 7:00 a.m., carrying all the New York and D.C. newspapers he was directed to read each morning to clip relevant articles and snippets of political interest to O'Brien and his district. He would remain there until the office opened at 9:00 a.m., then bring his clippings to O'Brien's legislative aide to review.

The Washington heat and humidity astonished Medici, who as a Long Islander thought he knew humidity, but nothing like this. The coolness of the Rayburn Building and the tunnels connecting it to the Capitol kept them inside and out of the heat all day, and Medici usually worked until 7:00 p.m. so that the heat would have abated some for the drive back up Connecticut Avenue to 19th and S Streets.

Some days he would have to go out. On Holy Days of Obligation he would drive O'Brien and Tip O'Neill to mass at a D.C. church so the good Irish Catholics and Medici could do their ecclesiastical duty.

At 19th and S off DuPont Circle he shared an old brownstone

with seven other Princetonians, all interns or law students. He never ate dinner there because it was so hot, and the communal refrigerator was always a quarter full of peanut butter jars and moldy cold cuts. Sometimes Mr. O'Brien would take him to dinner to meet lobbyists, arms dealers and other Members of Congress. Sometimes he would appear in O'Brien's stead at foreign embassy receptions for free eats and drinks, until the time at the Taiwanese Embassy reception when he ate 1,000 year old eggs and barfed in the parking lot.

Tonight he only had to do his laundry, so he drove back to the brownstone at 7:30 p.m., grabbed his laundry bag and headed on foot to the local laundromat, a crummy joint on the northeast side of Connecticut Avenue. There was a clear delineation between "browntown"— the African-American side of the avenue— and the white neighborhood: Afro-Americans on the southwest side, whites on the northeast side. The closest laundromat was for whites-only, a pigsty with two inches of soapy water and soggy dryer lint on the floor all the time, with broken, rusty machines. It was always full of young white folk who worked on the Hill.

This time the mess was too much for Medici. The place disgusted him even to enter, so he left disappointed and walked up Connecticut Avenue toward his room, carrying his full laundry bag on his back like Santa Claus.

At a stop light he looked across the broad lanes of Connecticut Avenue and spied another laundromat, apparently empty. Rather than search the Yellow Pages for another one, he darted across the avenue dodging traffic to see if this laundromat was open.

He entered, and it was like a dream. This establishment was new, spotless and shiny, with gleaming stainless steel machines, an immaculate floor, furniture and tables to fold laundry. But why was it empty?

He turned and the owner smiled at him, a tiny, grandmotherly, gray-haired black woman in a neat housedress who was always in attendance and kept the place spotless.

Medici said "Good evening," asked her for change and began to place all his dirty clothes in a new washer.

The lady said "You shouldn't mix colored clothes with your whites."

Medici shrugged. "I don't have time to do two loads, ma'am."

The lady came over and started separating the white clothes and putting them in a second washer.

"If you'll just leave me the money, I'll wash both loads, dry them and fold them for you. You can be on your way and come back in a couple of hours and I'll have them ready for you."

Medici's jaw dropped. Speechless for a moment, he smiled a big smile, said "Yes, Ma'am!" and gave her the money and a bit more. He strode out of the laundromat buoyant.

The next day at lunch in the Rayburn cafeteria he told the interns at the table about the new laundromat and the nice lady. Two southerners were appalled that he would patronize an establishment "clearly meant for darkies." One left the table.

Walking upstairs to O'Brien's office he remembered his mother, a woman of entirely Sicilian ancestry, proudly telling her sons that because of the historical conquests of Sicily its gene pool was strong because it contained Greek, Roman, Norse, Celt, African, Byzantine, Muslim-Arab, Norman, Lombard, Hohenstaufer, Catalan, Spanish and French stock. How could people be upset to use an African-American laundromat? He realized this was his first practical lesson in racism, and he didn't understand it.

Washington D.C. 1966

THE BREAKFAST CLUB

It was so late in the morning you could smell the day's batch of Navy Bean Soup cooking behind the swinging doors to the kitchen. The House Democratic Dining Room was empty save its solitary round table. At it sat one 80, four 60, and one 20 year old man. This was the infamous "Breakfast Club" at which the work of the House of Representatives was reportedly accomplished. The 20 year old sat as an intern to one of the sixties.

The oldest and the youngest at the table were stone silent. The youngest couldn't keep his eyes off the oldest, the Speaker of the House of Representatives. He appeared to be a cadaver. His skin was waxen, translucent, almost radiating cold.

His eyes, when open above half-mast, showed the lights were on, but that was all. The short cigar butt in his mouth looked three days old, and the only sign of life was his slow shaky hand rising to remove the cigar three or four times an hour. The most powerful man in the Legislative Branch of the great republic said not a damn word all morning.

Not that there weren't things to discuss. The others were the four senior majority members of the Rules Committee. Between them they represented the four quadrants of the nation and could bottleneck or stampede any legislation headed for the House floor.

They bantered:

"Will that Texan sonofabitch President win the war soon?"

"Why do all Texans have brown eyes?"

"Because they're full of shit."

"What if you see one with blue eyes?"

"He's low a quart."

Would (William O.) 'Red' Douglas retire from the Supreme

Court? Did you hear he had a pacemaker installed? Only problem, they put it on the wrong organ.

Would that little Mick sonofabitch Bobby Kennedy actually make a run for LBJ's Presidency?

Did ya hear LBJ wanted to make Bobby ambassador to Dallas?

Would Teddy Kennedy with his soft-spoken charm make a go for the Presidency when he grew up?

Minor mention of (Adam Clayton) 'Clayte' Powell's latest public works bill and some Midwestern freshman's resolution condemning our participation in Viet Nam.

A bell rang just outside the dining room door, and a white-clad Negro steward appeared at the round table and said, "Gentlemen, the Executive Session of the Rules Committee is about to begin."

The four Rules members rose to their feet in the greatest demonstration of effort seen that morning. They variously shuffled, hobbled or lumbered their way across the dining room. The young man watched them from the round table, then saw the Speaker raise a bony hand to his mouth ever so slowly, remove the cigar like a slick, wet cork from an old bottle and say, just above a hoarse whisper, "Boys."

The four stopped in their tracks. All eyes turned to the Speaker, who by now was rolling slow circles with his cigar hand, in an obvious effort to jog his memory about what he intended to say.

"Boys," he repeated, sounding anomalously like Mae West, the cigar tracing small, slow orbits before him, "Get out some rules."

Washington DC 1966

LESSON: HOW TO DEAL WITH AUTHORITY

Medici walked from the House dining room to Congressman O'Brien's office. Ms. Hicks, O'Brien's white-haired Administrative Assistant— they all called each other by their formal last names in O'Brien's office— sat at her typewriter in the reception office efficiently typing letters and answering the congressman's phone when it rang. Unlike many other congressmen and senators who kept large staffs, O'Brien had only one administrative and one legislative assistant and a single summer intern. As a result Medici and the two staff assistants rattled around in the congressman's huge suite of offices in the new Rayburn House Office Building. And to tell the truth, there really wasn't much to do.

There was a pending bill O'Brien had introduced on Food and Drug Administration that would require years of manufacturers' testing before new products which came in contact with the human body could be placed on the market. The FDA was O'Brien's sweet spot. In 1955 he had discovered in hearings that many lipsticks sold contained harmful carcinogens and were never tested before they were marketed, so O'Brien had introduced legislation that forced FDA to test cosmetics before they would be approved for sale to the public. Now, 11 years later, the issue was all the more poignant to O'Brien because his wife was dying of cancer.

Of course, the war in Vietnam was a constant irritant, and President Johnson regularly called the members of the House Rules Committee to strong-arm them to release the War Funding bill to the floor, as well as the Civil Rights Fair Housing Act— part of Johnson's Great Society initiative. The "Judge"— Congressman

Howard W. Smith of Virginia, a senior Rules Committee member and its recent chairman— had held up the Fair Housing bill because he wanted the act to exclude buildings of 25 or fewer dwelling units. Many of his contributor constituents were landlords of such apartments who feared "no white folk would rent from them if they had to rent even one unit to nigrahs."

O'Brien, a 280-pound former Golden Gloves boxer with knees crippled by arthritis, shuffled through the front door and bellowed "Where the hell's my intern?"

Medici jumped up from his typewriter where he was trying to draft an answer to 78 nearly identical letters from constituents of O'Brien's district which basically said "Get us out of Vietnam now!" While vocal, this group was a small minority in the district. The great weight of political sentiment in the completely Democratic district was to "bomb the North Vietnamese back to the Stone Age." O'Brien always laughed about the sentiment in his blue collar Italian and Irish district, calling himself a "secret Republican" because of the district's conservative leanings.

"Come in to my office!" O'Brien yelled. Medici followed the lumbering O'Brien into his spacious office whose huge windows framed the Capitol dome. O'Brien pointed to a chair in front of the desk and Medici sat.

"LBJ is really leaning on us to vote out the Fair Housing bill with a jurisdictional exclusion for buildings of four or fewer units. Judge Smith wants 25 or fewer units excluded in the bill. What do you think?"

Medici remembered the research from the Congressional Research Service.

"CRS says an exclusion of 25 or fewer units from the Fair Housing requirements would allow landlords of most of the South— and the country— to refuse to rent to African-Americans. Doesn't sound appropriate or fair to me."

"Yeah, but Judge Smith thinks he will be defeated this fall by money from the landlords' group in his Virginia district if the exclusion is only for four or fewer units."

Medici shrugged. "I'd say that's Judge Smith's problem. The 14th

Amendment says what it says— without any exclusion threshold."

O'Brien peered at Medici over the desk. "Easy for you to say, Princeton. But this is a big deal in the South. I'd hate to lose Judge Smith from Rules. He's a sage head."

Medici shrugged his shoulders.

"Okay. How you coming on the response to the anti-war letters from the district?"

Medici cleared his throat. "I'm almost done. I'm trying to show sympathy for their angst about the war, but remind them that we have lost a disproportionately large number of soldiers from our blue collar district, and that to ensure they haven't died in vain we must prevail in Vietnam to keep communism at bay in Southeast Asia."

O'Brien waved with a downward motion indicating he had heard enough. "That's fine. I would have been more terse myself."

Medici laughed. "Your legislative assistant Mr. Abbott and I played with that, too. Our best shot was 'Dear Anti-War Protestor: Buzz off!'"

O'Brien laughed.

"Well, we've got to come up with a position on this Fair Housing bill. LBJ's been calling the senior members of Rules almost daily trying to strong arm us to a four-unit exclusion— and to vote out the War Funding bill." O'Brien shook his head. "He's irritating and relentless! I'm not going to talk to him anymore until as a Committee we decide what to do."

The intercom buzzed on O'Brien's desk console. He punched a button.

"Mr. O, the President on the phone for you."

O'Brien shook his huge head and bellowed so he could be heard throughout the suite and down the hall, "Tell the President to go fuck himself!" He clicked off the intercom and smiled an impish smile.

Medici was stunned. It never occurred to him that anyone in government would refer to the powerful President that way. But he liked the exhilaration of insulting and ignoring power.

O'Brien winked at Medici. "Heavy-handed Texas sonofabitch. Let him sweat."

[The House Rules Committee voted out the Fair Housing bill to the House floor with the four unit exclusion, and it was passed into law. Congressman Howard W. Smith was defeated in the 1966 Virginia Democratic primary by liberal Democrat George Rawlings, Jr, who was defeated in the general election by Republican William L. Scott.]

Washington, DC 1966

THE LAST TIME I SAW BOBBY

Medici drove his 1961 Rambler carefully through the gate at Hickory Hill. He was astonished how quickly Washington turned rural on the way out of town toward McClean. The security guard stopped them and asked them to see their invitations.

"Thomas Medici, intern to Congressman Jim O'Brien, Ninth District, Queens, New York," he said.

"Sara Petoffsky, intern to Senator Jacob Javits of New York," Sara said.

The guard waved them through. They parked and walked toward the sprawling house, and were diverted to the entrance facing the huge back grounds, where Ethel Kennedy greeted them graciously with a warm smile. Bobby was nowhere to be seen at his annual party for all the interns of the members of the New York Delegation. Mostly, that meant his interns, since most of the offices had only one or two, but Bobby had 32. Many were students dedicated to reform, some just political groupies.

Medici and Sara got glasses of lemonade, then strolled the grounds. Neither of their bosses thought much of Bobby. Medici's congressman, a strong urban Democrat and former Golden Gloves champ, always referred to him as "that sawed-off son-of-a-bitch." The father of Medici's college roommate had attended Concord Academy with Bobby, and only remembered stuffing him butt first into a janitor's rolling trash receptacle. Apparently Bobby wasn't popular there.

Medici and Sara reached the tennis court. Two racquets hung in the net above a can of balls. They looked at each other and thought "Why not?" They picked up the racquets and began to volley in their business suits.

They heard the cry of the crowd and dozens of interns ran to the back doorstep of the mansion. There at the top of the steps stood Bobby with his signature shock of hair and toothy smile.

Sara said "Do you want to go meet him?"

"No," Medici said. "But go on up if you want."

Sara declined and they continued to volley.

"Nice forehand." Medici heard a voice behind him. He turned and there was Bobby, suit jacket open, hands in his pockets, smiling at them.

Medici didn't know what to say. Sara had dropped her racquet and came around the net. She introduced herself and shook the senator's hand.

Medici was astonished Bobby would leave the adulation of the groupie interns to walk down to the court to meet them. Bobby turned to him and said "Who do you work for?"

Medici extended his hand. Bobby was nothing like the SOB he had always heard him described.

"Tom Medici. I'm the sole intern for Jim O'Brien, Ninth District, Queens. Rules Committee."

"My brother Jack knew Jim well. Jim was very helpful in Jack's campaign in 1960."

"I know. Mr. O'Brien recites those stories often," Medici said. They were still shaking hands. Medici saw that there was something religiously charismatic about Bobby. But there was something else, something marked and tragic about the man. It was palpable, but Medici had never encountered it before, and wouldn't until four years later as a naval officer on the Cambodian border. It was the air of guys in the combat zone you knew were going to get killed. But he didn't realize that at the tennis court at Hickory Hill.

They chatted for a while longer, then Bobby walked up to the house, changed clothes, and the last time Medici saw him Bobby was wearing black pegged pants, black pointy shoes and a fuzzy powder-blue mohair sweater, driving a 1966 Pontiac Bonneville convertible out the driveway, headed for Georgetown bars with his brother Teddy and two family friends.

Medici remembered all this in June 1968 on the gun line in

Vietnam aboard USS TULSA, when the ship's public address system announced that Senator Robert Kennedy had been shot and killed in Los Angeles after winning the California Presidential Primary.

Washington DC 1966

TWIN STINGERS

"Coffee, Mr. Medici?" asked the short black man. The white starched collar of his steward's jacket captured Medici's attention: It was exactly like the one worn by the naval officer in the photograph in the *Naval Institute Proceedings* on his lap. It showed an admiral in Saigon in dress whites awarding a posthumous Navy Cross to a riverboat coxswain killed while rescuing an army patrol under fire from a riverbank in the Mekong delta. The steward wore the same coat without brass buttons or insignia.

Medici accepted the gleaming white porcelain cup from the steward and thanked him with a smile. He glanced around the living room of the Princeton Magna Carta Club. A jolly fire burned in the medieval fireplace, its roaring flames glinted brightly off the polished brass scanzas and silver coffee urn. The walnut panels of the immense room were decked with swag and holly boughs in celebration of Christmas 1966. A fragrant blue spruce dominated one corner of the living room, bejeweled with bright ornaments that twinkled as the flames crackled. The golden hue of the flames bathed the thick red carpet and green leather furniture in a way that hypnotized him with comfort and privilege.

Thomas Medici, Princeton senior, felt warm and cozy and not a little bit smug. Dinner in the candlelit club dining room had been satisfactory for a weekday. Despite the troubling photograph in the magazine on his lap, and the vague discomfort and excitement when they watched nightly "warflicks"— combat action scenes from Vietnam on the *CBS Evening News*— life was under control. No one in the club's senior section had been drafted, and now they were beginning to receive professional school acceptances and to plan June weddings. The war seemed at bay, thank God. He finished his coffee and headed back to his room to work on his senior thesis.

Medici stood in the hallway of his single room in 1903 Hall. He squinted as he scanned his mail in the dim light. His eyes riveted on one return address: LOCAL BOARD NO. 3, SECOND FLOOR, 1447 NORTHERN BLVD., MANHASSET, N.Y. 11030, his draft board. Instinctively he knew it was not a student deferment recertification form. His pulse quickened as he tore it open: It was a "Greetings" letter. He unlocked the door, turned on the light and sat at the desk, ashen. The calendar on the wall seemed to mock him with the cheery Christmas decorations encircling "December 1966."

Medici trembled as he read the letter. Senior year. Just turned twenty-one. Thesis not done, not even an outline. And now a goddam "Greetings" letter from his draft board. He had proposed to Nonie tentatively fourteen months ago during a football weekend and formally last summer, but he really hadn't the foggiest notion of how he would support her. He was in a real bind. And now Local Board Number 3 of Great Neck had jerked his 2-S student deferment and told him to report for his induction physical.

At first he didn't see how this was possible, they were supposed to let you finish your four years and get your degree. He had talked to his uncle who sat on the Board and found that the doctors and lawyers and matrons on the Board deferred everyone going to college from the bedroom suburbs of Long Island, and all the draft age kids went to college. So the Board had to cheat a little on the student deferments of the kids from the outlying clam digger towns like Harborville, Medici's home. His uncle neglected to tell him that the Board would honor a written medical excuse, however flimsy, from any bumpkin doctor for a permanent 4-F medical deferment. But his uncle had served briefly in World War I and, as a patriotic, childless second generation Italian-American, he held certain firm beliefs. He believed he could not ethically divert his nephew from service required by the country that had given the Medici family the opportunity to succeed on this continent rather than starve on the returns of hardscrabble farming in Calabria. So now Medici held his induction letter.

He thumbed through the *Naval Institute Proceedings* addressed to his roommate Jeb. Jeb was pulling all the strings he could for a waiver to get *into* the navy due to his poor eyesight. The magazine talked of destroyers and cruisers and the imminent refurbishment of the battleship New Jersey for service in Vietnam. A long detailed article described combat watercraft of Vietnam, PCFs and PBRs— the navy's dual diesel, jacuzzi drive, riverine patrol boats for the shallow waterways of the Mekong Delta. A picture accompanying the article showed a camouflaged sailor in a turret on a PCF Swiftboat, arm slung over "twin stingers"— dual fifty calibre machine guns, mystically feared by the Viet Cong and the North Vietnamese Army because of the horrid destruction they inflicted.

He drummed his fingers on the large desk he had constructed from a blank hollow-core door— it sagged from the weight of his thesis research and amplified the finger drumming like far off infantry on the march. They pay you in the navy, he thought. I could save up some money for law school and Nonie could get her graduate degree and work wherever I am stationed. That will take care of the support problem.... He resolved to call the local navy recruiter in the morning to see what the deal was.

The dim light of a single 60-watt bulb transformed the room's shabbiness to elegant disrepair, like a hotel in a Graham Greene novel. He walked a few steps and stumbled as his foot caught a yarn loop of the ancient threadbare rug. The lobby was bad enough with all the homosexuals milling around casting discrete glances at anyone who entered. But the price was right at nine dollars a night in the Philadelphia YMCA, and it stood across the street from the Thirteenth Street Naval Station where Medici had his Officer Candidate School exams and interview in the morning. He took his dopp kit and towel down the hall to shower and shave so he could roll out early for the 7 A.M. physical.

"Juntullmuns," Gunnery Sergeant Garcia said to the nine potential officer candidates, "if youse will kindly move behind the partition we will throughput today's load of draftees." Medici couldn't believe how *polite* everyone had been.

Medici and his small group walked behind the half partition. Their legs and tops of their heads extended below and above it. By standing on his toes Medici could see what was happening in the large, cold room.

The swinging doors flew open. Garcia shouted: "All right, you gorillas, get your butts in here along the dotted yellow lines, drop your skivvies, bend over and pull your cheeks apart so the doc can check you for hemorrhoids!" The "gorillas"— mostly black men and a few grossly overweight Slavic-Americans— shuffled in like so many cattle. Two long lines of them, about 120 in number eventually ambled in and, with prodding from Garcia, assumed the position for the inspection. They stood bent over in the awkward position fully ten minutes, some shaking visibly from the harsh February cold, before a white-coated doctor in surgical gloves strode in with a clipboard and a tube of KY Jelly. He walked behind the rows of men, up and down, not looking at their rumps, rather reading the clipboard in his left hand. When he got to the last man in the second row, he stopped short, absent-mindedly put some jelly on his middle finger, and without bending down or looking at his target, shoved the finger into the black man's anus. The man leaped from the floor and let out a croak. The doc looked at Garcia and both smirked.

"All pass with flying colors, Sergeant," the doc yelled over his shoulder on his way out the door.

His physical and written exams completed, Medici waited in a shabby conference room with eight potential officer candidates. The navy was taking less than fifty percent of OCS applicants these days since so many draft candidates were trying to escape the army to the more benign naval service. Medici's father had always told him the best part about the navy was that regardless of what they did to you during the day at war, you usually got a hot meal, hot shower, and clean sheets afterward.

They waited for the all-important interview with the recruiting officer. No matter what your test scores were like, the recruiting officer had the absolute final say whether the navy wanted you or not— if he liked the "cut of your jib." He might offer as a consolation prize a four-year stint as an enlisted man with low pay, lousy accommodations, and the likelihood of being sent as a PBR gunner on the jungle rivers of Vietnam.

Medici noticed the crew was extremely nervous as he looked around the conference table. They were mostly scared wimps he concluded. One was obviously at least thirty. Medici watched him carefully.

"I'm Doctor David Rankin," the man said.

"I'm Tom Medici," he said, offering his hand.

"I'm a plastic surgeon— tits and ass," he giggled nervously. "I'm trying to get into the navy because I got my draft notice. I have this one shot and that's it. Otherwise I come through again with the gorillas to report for active duty. Or go to Canada." He laughed weakly, then paused, looks of disgust then fear crossing his face. "This Vietnam war really sucks, y'know?"

Medici thumbed a torn copy of the *Naval Institute Proceedings*. It was the same one he had seen with the article about the navy's riverine forces in Vietnam. He turned quickly to the picture of the dual fifty-calibre machine guns and threw the magazine on the table in front of Rankin.

"Twin stingers," Medici said loudly, startling the waiting candidates. "I wanna kill gooks with twin stingers— TUH-TUH-TUH, TUH-TUH-TUH!" Medici held up his fists as if he were shooting big fifty-calibre slugs around the table, baiting them. He stifled a laugh. "Just let me sign on the dotted line," he rhymed.

Rankin moved away from him to an empty chair and the silence returned. The office door opened and a naval lieutenant in dress blues with a file in his hand approached the table and said, "Thomas Medici."

Princeton 1967

And After...

IV. Paris
1982

FROM SHAKESPEARE AND CIE'S LIBRARY

Outside the window, the spring greenery of an enormous elm began to glow as if a religious vision, intruding upon the night. Spellbound, Medici stared at it long seconds, not understanding what he saw. The green shimmering continued for a quarter-minute, then disappeared abruptly. The quiet sound of the Seine lapping gently against its banks reached his ears and comprehension, like water, seeped slowly back into his mind. A *bateau mouche* hidden by the quay wall had cast its searchlights behind the tree, then passed slowly downriver under the Pont St. Michel, breaking the spell and returning the night's dark peace.

Paris 1982

LES ANCIENS DE L'INDOCHINE

Medici's first night in Paris found him in L'Archestrate in the 7th Arrondissement, a small restaurant decorated with cane wallpaper, chocolate browns, and terra cotta. The maître d', a Gallic bantam in best Parisian form, pretended not to understand anything Medici ordered. He persisted in standing with his order pad in front of him, shaking his head "non" with each question Medici asked or item he tried to order. Finally Medici shouted, turning all the heads in the restaurant.

"Quel est votre problème, monsieur? Avez-vous un maladie de l'oreille? Vous devriez les nettoyer plus souvent. Allez-vous prendre ma commande, ou est que j'ai besoin de parler plus fort?" *What is the matter with you, sir? Do you have a malady of the ears? You should clean them more often. Will you take my order or do I need to speak louder?*

The maître d' withered in size. He looked around the restaurant at the annoyed patrons, several saying "Servez lui!" *Serve him!*

Medici whispered in French his order for nettle soup and sole meunière, and miraculously the maître d' caught every word.

After dinner Medici strolled to the Vietnamese section of the 7th, closer to the Seine. He had read about an avant-garde restaurant and bar called Le Mot— *The Word.*

He sat at the bar, ordered an Armagnac and chatted with the friendly bartender. The smell of *pho* and *cha gio* coming from the kitchen comforted him. He was among friends here.

The restaurant door flew open with a noise like a shot. Medici turned and spied an Oscar Wilde look-alike moving expansively through the doorway.

"Moi, j'y suis!" *I'm here!* The man shouted as he loped toward the bar. He was older, Medici guessed nearly 50, but was trim and very pale skinned. Dressed completely in black, his longish hennaed hair flowed over his collar, and he carried his left arm in an ostentatious sling made of a brightly colored Pucci scarf. Medici thought it an affectation, until he saw the mangled left hand grotesquely healed from some ancient wound.

The man asked the bartender "Qui est-il?" *Who is he?*

"Un Américain, Marcel." *An American, Marcel.*

"Ah— un Amércain— un 'Rican!'" *Ah— an American— a 'richey'*, said Marcel, lighting a Gauloise cigarette.

"Peût-etre qu'il va me payer un verre?" *Maybe he'll buy me a drink?*

The bartender waved Marcel off, shook his palms and his head "Non."

Medici said "Certainment! Garcon, un Armagnac pour monsieur Marcel." *Certainly! Bartender, an Armagnac for Mister Marcel.*

Marcel sat two stools from Medici. The bartender brought his drink.

"Vous me semble triste, monsieur. Pourquoi?" *You seem sad to me, sir. Why?*

"Pas de raison: Un divorce récent; congédié de mon travaille en tant qu'avocat. La vie est généralement de merde. *No reason: A recent divorce, fired from my job as a lawyer. Life is generally shitty.*

"Je sympathise avec vous. Je suis passé par qu'il y a des années quand je suis rentré de Dien Bien Phu. J'étais le plus jeune officier la quand nous avons cédé. Il a rendu ma vie misérable pendant des années." *I sympathize with you. I went through that years ago, when I returned from Dien Bien Phu. I was the youngest officer there when we surrendered. It made life miserable for me for years.*

Medici perked up. "Dien Bien Phu? Were you Legion?"

"*Am Legionnaire, monsieur!* Once and always!" Marcel said in accented English. Marcel hoisted his drink in a salute. Medici returned the salute with his snifter.

"I am, too. Vietnam veteran from our war."

"Monsieur! I knew we have something in commons. Nous sommes Les Anciens de L'Indochine."

"What?" said Medici.

Again in broken English, Marcel said "Old Timers of Indochina. It take me many years to appreciate the tître. It was what they called us, the survivors of Dien Bien Phu."

"I like the sound of that. 'Les Anciens de L'Indochine.' You French have a nice way of putting things. 'Les Anciens de L'Indochine.' Sounds like a sacred order, or a knighthood." Medici laughed.

"Comment vous appellez-vous?" *What's your name?*

"Thomas."

A waitress walked by the bar with a baguette of French bread. Marcel stood and grabbed it. He stood over Medici and with a formal deliberate motion raised the baguette like a king's knighting sword and touched each of Medici's shoulders.

"Je vous chevalie 'Chevalier Thomas, un Ancien de L'Indochine.'" *I knight thee 'Sir Thomas, Old Timer of Indochina.*

Medici laughed and bowed gracefully. Marcel returned the bread to the waitress and said "S'il vous plait, n'oubliez pas de cet ordre sacré au fil des ans! Merci pour le verre." *Please don't forget this sacred order over the years! Thanks for the drink.*

Medici laughed and felt an enormous weight lifted from his shoulders. Marcel tossed down the last of his Armagnac, saluted Medici with his good hand, and walked out the door with a flourish.

Paris 1982

TRUNG

Trung, Medici's net handler, doesn't look much different at forty-five than he did at thirty-two in Ha Tien. His tapered oval face looks sallow. Huge pockmarks, scars of pockmarks, and freckles make him appear not quite Asian, not quite European. Medici had reported in an aside that the few times he met Trung, the man picked his face constantly. He still does. He begins:

"I knew LT Medici. The American paid well. From the beginning he had an obsession with Cambodia far out of proportion to what was going on there militarily. He insisted on more and more Cambodian intelligence— military, political, whatever. He was the boss, and paid well, so I gave him what he wanted. I extended the coverage of the Collection Team 5 network all the way up the Cambodian coast to Thailand by the time he was MEDEVAC. I used fishermen who plied the coast that far north to report. Some of their stuff was way off base, really speculative, but they did report elements of the 101st NVA regiment in the vicinity of Sihanoukville a year before anyone in Saigon would believe it.

"The coastal infiltration of VC weapons by motorized junks and fishing boats was another example of giving him what he wanted. One night he saw what he thought was a flashing light from a fishing boat answered by a flashing light from Nui Sa Ky mountain. Apparently a riverboat went out and grabbed the boat, but a search showed no weapons, nothing. So I made up a whole line of reports about Chinese trawlers beaching at Kep and offloading considerable amounts of weapons, and small fishing boats infiltrating them down into Vietnam's waters to deliver to the VC. I remember the trawler name I made up— 'Hundred Flowers.' I heard it on the BBC World Service broadcast. It was the Chinese name for their supposed policy of artistic freedom." Trung laughs and lights another Gauloise Blanc. He smokes incessantly.

"The biggest offering I made toward his Cambodian fetish was A-34, the recording secretary of the Cambodian cabinet. This guy was *un pédé* and promiscuous in every way. Why, he was a TRIPLE agent— for the North Vietnamese, the Americans, and for the Cambodians so they would know about the other two countries' collection capabilities and plant disinformation helpful to Cambodia. One example of disinformation was the report that Lon Nol had idealistically turned down the offer of the Chinese to kill his old opponent Prince Sihanouk if he would continue to allow ships carrying Chinese weapons to unload at Sihanoukville. Agent A-34 reported this and Medici and the Americans lapped it up as proof of the idealism and political loyalty of the new Lon Nol government. What A-34 didn't report was that the PRC simply couldn't meet Lon Nol's bribe price but the CIA could!"

Trung laughs nervously at this last revelation and draws deeply on his cigarette. He is beginning to sweat now although we sit in my air-conditioned hotel room at Antibes, paid for by the *LA Times*, where Trung has come from Marseille for this interview, for a price, of course.

"What was ever more clever was the way I introduced A-34 to Medici. He didn't have the imagination to seek the recruitment of a highly placed agent, and I thought he might be suspicious if A-34 just appeared among the fishermen and woodcutters of his network. So I made an arrangement with Frank Brown's net handler— Frank was the Army Intelligence guy in Ha Tien— to recruit A-34. I knew Brown and Medici worked closely, and that Medici had the authority to draw political conclusions in his reports about Lon Nol's loyalty, which the Army never would let Brown do." He giggles nervously, almost like a scared schoolgirl. "A-34 paid me $10,000 U.S. to become the American's best Cambodian agent!

"Medici got the ear of those in Saigon. They went nuts over all the Cambodian stuff he sent them. I think it was out of boredom with the rest of the war. They flipped to Cambodia as if it were the latest TV show on a new channel, even though it really wasn't that important to the war, other than the way it caused domestic dissension in the U.S. The American command shifted its attention like changing channels. I was in an American military club in Can Tho once and they had one of those TVs with the remote control. It drove me crazy the way all they did was flip between channels; they never saw more than a fleeting scene of any show. They were the same way with intelligence issues: Cambodia was a more interesting if less relevant channel.

"Anyway, I lessened reporting of weapons shipments across the Vinh Te canal, even though those infiltrations had increased dramatically between north-south grid lines VS 60-90— the middle of the canal— when the U.S. pulled out its river patrol boats in that sector, halfway between Chau Doc and Ha Tien. You see, we were trying to get as much stuff across as we could before the inevitable Cambodian invasion occurred. The Americans paid little or no attention to the Vinh Te canal; after Medici started traveling in Cambodia he didn't even brief the boat captains anymore on likely crossing points and so forth. As long as there was no contact on the river and no Americans getting shot, no one minded. Meanwhile we were infiltrating massive amounts of weapons and ammo out of Cambodia into Vietnam. The tantalizing but unimportant Cambodia information kept Medici and his superiors preoccupied. When they found little ammo and weaponry in Cambodia during the invasion it was not because it had been moved further into Cambodia away from the border, but because it had already been infiltrated into Vietnam. They were on a romantic wild goose chase!"

"Medici's idea to pay the agents in Cambodian riels instead of inflated Vietnamese piastres was really good— especially for me. I drew pay as net handler plus pay for two agents that I invented! The CIA paid me even more than Medici did for rewritten versions of the same reports I gave him."

"I received very little pay from the North Vietnamese, but I rose to the rank of colonel in the Viet Cong, and I still draw a tiny pension for my service. I worked for them mostly because a U.S. Special Forces team interrogated and left my mother for dead when they first arrived in 1961. That had an effect on my sympathies." He croaks a nervous laugh.

"I was able to retire to Dalat when the north rolled south in 1975, but with the money I made over ten years from the Americans, I moved to my mother's hometown of Aix-en-Provence here in the Midi. I knew I had people there. I help provide for my mother and her family and write fiction for the local newspaper at five cents a word. Not as lucrative as I got in Vietnam for my intelligence reports, but not bad for France." He smiles and lights another cigarette.

"Lieutenant Medici won't read this, will he?" Trung laughs a nervous laugh.

Antibes 1983

OBITUARY OF TRUNG, ANH LE

La Provençal (newspaper of Marseille, France)

Necrologies: 3 Mars 1984

Trung, Anh Le, 46
M. Trung est mort au trois Mars quand, a l'improviste, son auto a perdue les freins sur le Haut Corniche vers Cap Ferrat.

M. Trung a été un écrivant pour quelques périodiques françaises régionales depuis son arrivé a Aix-en-Provence à 1978. Il est né au Vietnam en 1938.

Dons et fleurs seront acceptés par son mère, Mme Trung, à 13 Rue Catinat, Aix-en-Provence.
Marseilles 1984

La Provencal (newspaper of Marseilles, France)

Obituaries: 3 March 1984
Trung, Anh Le, 46
Mr. Trung died on March 3d, when his automobile unexpectedly lost its brakes while he drove the High Corniche road toward Cap Ferrat.

Mr. Trung was a writer for several French regional periodicals after his arrival at Aix-en-Provence in 1978. He was born in Vietnam in 1938.

Donations and flowers will be accepted by his mother, Madame Trung, at 13 rue Catinat, Aix-en-Provence.

Marseilles 1984

V. Del Mar and Princeton
Or, The Surprise Bachelorhood
1983

NVA DREAM

It's four o'clock in the morning. May 2, 1984. I've just awakened from one of those vivid dreams. I was sitting on a large bamboo platform; it must have been half as large as a football field. With me were some of my Vietnam buddies like Frank Brown, the army intelligence guy. We were looking across a gap and there, against another bamboo wall, within clear sight so you could identify their facial features, were a whole group of North Vietnamese soldiers.

As the dream started we were talking amongst ourselves then noticing that the North Vietnamese soldiers— they wore khaki green uniforms with double-ended pith helmets— very rapidly and efficiently were setting up a 106mm mortar on its base, then they launched a round in our direction. You could actually watch the onion shaped bomb in mid air. I remember grabbing a broken down M79 grenade launcher and running toward the other end of the platform, away from where the rounds would land. All I knew was that I had to get there and start shooting rounds at the mortar team who were launching at us, regardless of whether they shot at me or not.

The realization I had in this dream was that the event for which I got a Bronze Star, and which I underplay whenever anybody asks me about it, scared the shit out of me. In that event we were driving north on the dike road, Route 8A from Ha Tien into Cambodia, and I had my army intelligence friend Frank Brown and someone else in my jeep. As I was driving past the RuffPuff hill outpost, I noticed mortar rounds going off quite close to us, down off the road in the paddies on the approach to the outpost.

It's interesting reliving just that one moment as you're driving fifty miles an hour down the road, seeing rather than hearing mortar rounds go off. It was interesting to try to decide what to do. Do you pull off and go to the left? I think what I did was to find the next road off to the left and get out of the jeep with our rifles and PRC-25 radio and hide behind the dike which was about as much protection as we could get out there in the middle of the paddy. We stayed there for nine hours while our little outpost at Phao Dai called in tactical air support. We were at the end of the line— it was just about as far as you could get from Saigon— and had never received much tactical air support for any problems along the border. This time they considered it a tactical emergency because we were Americans pinned down on the Cambodian border. And while we were waiting for the initial air strikes, all we asked for from our outpost was an M79 grenade launcher and some fried chicken.

I remember three or four of us in the corner made by the dike roads in a paddy out in the middle of nowhere, no support around us as it got dark. The M79, and the extent to which my friend could use an M-16— which wasn't much— would have been our only security had they come at us from any direction, not just from the mountain under bombardment. We knew we were in no man's land out there because the Viet Cong roamed the area with impunity after 4 pm every day. And all we had was the M79 and the M-16, and I felt responsible for the lives of the guys I was with.

Fortunately nothing worse happened. Some local peasants sort of hung around us, which probably frightened us all the more because we didn't know whose side they were on, or if this was a set up. It was just past the harvest and a huge pile of rice stalks stood one hundred yards behind us. After dark someone— bad guys— somehow set it afire and the huge blaze illuminated our positions from behind. You could see us from a mile away. So we were kind of sitting ducks up against this dike wall corner. We were just waiting to get hit, but fortunately we didn't.

I think in the dream there was an instant recognition of seeing those mortar rounds coming, and knowing you had to hit them back somehow. In the dream the M79 appeared to provide our security in the later part of the mortar episode.

I guess the net effect of this dream thirteen years after the fact is that a lot of these experiences that I pooh-pooh and underplay now were really frightening at the time. I can tell particularly because I can feel it right in the pit of my stomach. My gut had been twisted up, and after surviving the dream, it relaxed and I calmed. I think that's what's occurred this past year, as I started to write the book on my spy time in Cambodia— a psychological memory of visceral fear.

Del Mar 1983

OUTCALL

"College Coeds Escort Service," the woman's voice said sweetly.

"Hi. Ahh, I'd like to engage your services tonight. Saw your ad in the Yellow Pages under Outcall Massage," Tom said.

"Ooh, great!"

A real bimbo, he thought happily.

"If you'll just give me your number I'll call right back."

"297-4162."

CLICK.

He cut himself a piece of his son's three-day-old chocolate birthday cake and was munching a mouthful when the phone rang.

"MMFUHWD," he said with a full mouth.

"Is this 297-4162?"

"Yup."

"College Coeds here. Now, have you used our services before?"

"Nope. I've never done this before. I just got separated last month and..."

"I understand. What are you eating?"

"Some of my son's birthday cake. Want some?" He liked her phone personality. "Tell me where you are and I'll bring it over."

"That's rad. I'd love some, but not now. I guess you haven't heard our spiel yet."

"No."

"Well, we offer three specialized services. First, the Sorority, where your escort will dance naked from the waist up, and you may watch." She sounded awfully singsongy now, like a PSA stewardess.

"That's one hundred dollars. The second is the Cheerleader where your escort will dance with nothing on but leg warmers and you may help her undress. That's one hundred twenty dollars. And finally— I know this is the one you've been waiting for— the Best in the West, where your escort will dance totally nude, and you can dance with her!"

"Aah— I'd like to ask a discreet question— aah— "

"Yes— we're a full service, hands on operation."

"I guess I'll get the Cheerleader— how much was that?"

"One twenty."

"How much is the top of the line?"

"Best in the West? One fifty."

"Yeah, I think I'll get that."

"Fine. Now if you'll give me your name and address, we'll have your escort there within an hour."

Tom Medici. 124 Upas St. Number B."

"Thank you." She hung up.

An hour seemed a long time, Tom thought. Especially at 10 PM. He was already getting sleepy and the libido was slipping away, but even this state was better than the urgency that drove him to call in the first place. He didn't know what to do. Watch television? Play some good music? This wasn't exactly a date.

He decided to play Jobim's "Wave" album, and as the tone arm descended, he felt the need for a stiff drink. He poured Martell into a snifter, and it took him back thirteen years to Ha Tien, the dirty business and dirty tricks. The cognac rushed memories to the front of his consciousness, particularly the high state of intuition induced from living by your wits under combat stress.

He remembered clearly the moment of *gestalt* when something his subconscious had been toiling over came bursting through to consciousness at unlikely moments. Hackles bristling, he relived the time he nearly drove off a dike road, when he intuited the reason why his jeep but none of the others were fired upon near the Cambodian border. For convenience, a predecessor had applied small reflective yellow letters to the jeep's windscreen to differentiate it from army jeeps of the same color in the lot. NVA gunners, desirous of the cash prize for killing an intelligence officer, also spotted the letters with binoculars and fired whenever the jeep approached the border— until he scraped the letters off. The memory of the danger made him feel good, and he laughed about it as he warmed and mellowed with the cognac.

WEE DOO WEE DOO WEET, his Japanese phone warbled.

"Hullo."

"Mr. Med-a-chee. This is College Coeds. I'm sorry. We can't find verification of an address for you at 124 Upas."

"What?"

"Is it Medahchee, M-E-D-A-H-C-H-E-E?"

"No. M-E-D-I-C-I."

"Oh, let's see..."

He heard her thumb through a phone book.

"Here it is. Fine, Mr. Medici. Someone will be there in half an hour."

Jesus Christ, he thought. It's already been forty minutes. His libido had nearly fizzled. All this checking and cross-checking seemed unnecessary. He guessed they were making sure he had a valid address and was not calling from a storefront or motel that might be a vice squad setup for the girl. He remembered vice squad bozos from his time as a prosecutor. He was never sure who represented the greater evil, those who trafficked in sex for a living or the squad ghouls who steeped themselves in it twenty-four hours a day. The squad's women undercover cops were so zealous, they frequently solicited johns to the point where a jury could not tell who was more at fault, cop or customer, and the charges were thrown out as entrapment.

He paced back and forth in the dark kitchen, then stopped at the bay window and surveyed the quiet street. He sniffed and sipped his brandy and watched passing cars with renewed excitement, as if awaiting the arrival of a girl for a college weekend. He smiled at the unlikely comparison and shook his head. A car pulled up in front of his apartment.

He watched eagerly to see what she looked like. Instead of a woman, a chunky balding man in an overcoat— Arab or Lebanese with a bushy mustache— got out and walked to the apartment complex next to his. He relaxed. Who'd want a girl who drove a '60 Ford Falcon anyway, he thought.

He continued his quiet vigil, sipping the cognac, standing in the darkened window. A 280Z, a Porsche and a Celica all drove by slowly, but none stopped. Then from an entry of the apartments on the left, the man with the mustache returned to the Falcon, slid behind the wheel and sat there, unaware he was being watched. And he sat there some more...

Then it hit Medici, like the old days. The hair on the back of his neck stood up as his subconscious crashed through the cognac and screamed "Undercover vice cop— a setup!"

His blood surged as in Nam when recognition overtook *him* before the other guy's similar recognition. Back then, enough to kill before being killed.

He quickly went out the side door and down the dark path that led to the street ten feet behind the Falcon, in its blind spot. He stalked quietly until he was behind the driver's door. Then he rapped sharply twice on the window and caused the mustache to bolt up from a deep slouch. He worried briefly whether the cop was carrying a pistol, but reasoned that if undercover he would blow his stake out if he drew it.

"Evening, can I help you?" Medici said to the mustache in his best imitation of an officer stopping a motorist for a ticket.

"AAH— no. I'm just sitting here getting my head together."

"Is that right?" Medici said curtly. "May I see some identification?".

The incredulous look on the man's face told Medici everything. With some fumbling he produced a dog-eared driver's license from a clutch of soiled dollar bills. The car smelled yeasty.

Medici read the address on the license. "You don't live around here," he said.

"I got a friend who lives a few blocks over."

"This isn't a few blocks over," Medici taunted.

"No law against just sittin' here quiet."

"Well, we don't like it. We run a tight ship in this neighborhood. I suggest if you have no business here you move along before we call the cops."

"You a Neighborhood Watch guy or something?" the startled

driver mumbled.

"You got it," Medici said. "Now shove off."

"Ah, is your name Medahchee?" the driver asked as he started the ignition.

Medici nodded.

Shaking his head, the mustache slipped the car into gear.

The Falcon started to move. Medici called to the driver, "By the way, the Best in the West pitch she gave was entrapment. You'd be out of court on your ass."

The officer laughed and drove off.

Del Mar 1983

MEXICAN BORDER

As they reached the border crossing Medici could barely sit up straight in the back seat. The tequila had been excellent. Only a few miles before he had discovered that Rafael's two friends from San Francisco, Jay and Ed, were also Italian-American, they Abbruzzese, and they laughed and reveled about that. The portly young border guard eyed them suspiciously. Medici was the only one who looked foreign beside Guillermo, Rafael's driver, who was clearly Mexican.

"What are your nationalities, gentlemen," the guard asked. Guillermo answered politely, "Mexican."

Medici didn't like the guard's smug look, so he screamed, "The three of us are Italian, you fat turkey!"

The guard remained calm despite the insult, "May I see your passports, please?"

Medici freaked. "You jerk, no one needs a passport to get in and out of Mexico!" he shouted. The driver and the passengers were beginning to get nervous, knowing that the next stop would be a long, slow secondary search.

"You do if you're a foreign national," the guard responded accurately.

Medici started to climb across the back seat to better confront the guard. "How many Bronze Stars you got, asshole?" he shouted.

The guard clearly understood what Medici was talking about, that he was not a foreign national, and that he had too much to drink. He waved Guillermo through, giving up on the hopeless veteran, then yelled as they pulled away, pointing to Guillermo, "He's the only one who knows who he is. You guys don't. Make up your minds if you're Americans or not!"

Del Mar 1983

OFFICE HOURS

Office hours in the Woodrow Wilson School bored Medici. Usually no students came by to discuss Urban Politics, the high points of the hours being his acquaintance with Ahmed, the associate professor next door, an Arab-American from University of Michigan with whom he shared the distinction of having declined the invitation to work for CIA.

And Professor Robert Goheen, President of Princeton in 1963 when Medici was a high school senior. Goheen had locked down the campus, canceling Medici's visit, after the spring campus riots which Goheen famously characterized as "hooliganism," unwittingly insuring that Medici and other high school seniors with acceptances would attend Princeton. Goheen, raised the child of missionaries in India, and just returned from New Dehli as U.S. Ambassador, turned out to be a funny, interesting and humble man, internationalist in his outlook.

Not many students visited, but Medici expected some today since he posted mid-term exam grades. One of only two men in his precept section of fourteen had failed the mid-term. Two guys, twelve girls— not like the old Princeton. Truth was, the women were much more settled and serious students than the men at that age, no surprise to Medici.

Two sharp raps on his door.

"Come in."

Bo Barrigan filled the door frame. Medici watched as fleeting expressions crossed the football player's face— anger, contrition, haplessness, then a red flush.

"Sit down, Bo. What can I do for you?"

"Professor, I …. Well, I was wondering."

"…About you mid-term grade? You failed the test. In fact, you were the only one in the precept section to fail."

Bo's red turned brighter. Medici thought his face could light the room.

"See, professor, I'm on the football team, and that takes a lot of time in the fall semester…."

"I'm sure it does. So what?"

"Well, I was wondering if I could get my grade up. Maybe do some extra credit work, or write a paper…"

"Nope. You had plenty of time to prepare for the mid-term, and everything on the test was covered in detail in the lectures and precepts. You didn't even have to read much of the material to pass."

Bo fidgeted in his seat. Medici could see Bo's brain re-setting, calculating another approach.

"You're a lawyer from San Diego, right? My Dad's a partner in Hobbs & Barrigan in Irvine— that's where I'm from."

"Where did you go to high school, Bo?"

"College High in Irvine. I was valedictorian of my class."

"I see." Medici sat up straight and cleared his throat. "Bo, you've got to look at the big picture here. It's great that you play football on top of Princeton's demanding studies. It's keeping your plate full of good things— you know, the way the Jesuits teach.

"But it's no good to do extra curricular activities and abandon your studies. I know. I was on the sailing team as an undergraduate here, and never attended a Saturday morning French class because we were away at regattas. We won the Middle Atlantic championships, and placed well at the Nationals, but I got a 7— 'flagrant neglect'— in that French course, even though I was good at the language. I saw the professor ten years later as he lead the academic procession at my sister-in-law's graduation. I told him I had received a medal in the Navy for negotiating in French a secret weapons agreement with the Cambodian Navy during the Vietnam War. He smiled, looked at me and said 'Très bien, Monsieur Medici. See what happens when you do your homework!' He was right.

"Your studies are why you are here. This is not a Big Ten school where football is everything. If you're an athlete here, you are expected to be an athlete-scholar. Your studies will prepare your mind for law school or whatever graduate work you do."

Medici tapped the blotter in front of him.

"But more important, what you do here begins to prepare you for life. Don't you know why we load you up with so much reading in each course? You know that kids at most other colleges don't read half as much. We're trying to confirm you as a lifelong voracious reader, unafraid of daunting intellectual challenges or massive amounts of material to master after you leave."

Bo touched his fingers together in his lap, 'Here is the church, here is the steeple' style.

"There's a bigger issue. You're a smart guy. I know your high school. There haven't been enough Californians— especially southern Californians— attending Princeton. You have a responsibility, a reputation to uphold— actually, to create— for your school and our region. If you do well here academically, you pave the way for more acceptances to Princeton in the future."

Medici smiled. "Not to put too much on you, but try to remember that."

Bo nodded. He was paying attention. "But the mid-term grade…"

"Is what it is. It's only 25% of the course grade, so nail the final and you'll do fine."

His mission failed, Bo nodded again and rose.

"Are you playing on Saturday?" Medici asked.

"Yes. Penn. Here."

"Good. I'll be watching. Penn's generally a pushover."

Bo laughed, opened the door and left.

In February, after reading period, Medici read and graded the numbered anonymous exams. He placed them in piles of Gaussian distribution, only two of the 52 in the highest grade stack. He turned the exam grades into the registrar, got the decode sheet and discovered to his pleasure that Bo had received the second highest grade on the final, missing first by only one point. The discovery made the whole semester worthwhile.

Princeton 1983

DRAFT AGE

"You know it's really unfair that we can be drafted at eighteen but can't drink most places," Kevin said. The 22-year-old lifeguard's voice wavered.

"That's right," chimed Eleanor, a bleach blond, nuclear-freeze, save-the-whales, NPR type from the 'burbs. "It's grossly unfair and illogical to draft our youth to die but prevent them from having a beer!" she said, smugly assuming that the writer would be impressed by her fervent, rote liberalism.

"Perhaps unfair under some fuzzy value system, but not illogical," said the writer, focusing his icy hawk eyes on the blond. "In fact, if you analyze your proposition you're really saying that merely because males are theoretically subject to the draft at age eighteen, even though there has been no draft for years, they should immediately be permitted to drink alcoholic beverages and slaughter themselves on the highway. It makes no sense."

Kevin interjected. "My dad was 18 during the Korean war. When he flew home through San Francisco he was refused a beer because the drinking age was 21."

"That may be. But I'm willing to bet he got a drink somewhere in San Francisco and didn't go home dry," the writer said. "There never has been any real problem for combat veterans to be served alcohol somewhere. And that's the real basis of the wishy-washy argument about draft and drinking age: those actually drafted into combat fairly should not be deprived of the right to drink. It's not a theoretical proposition at all. Why should one who is only potentially subject to draft, if there were a draft, be rewarded with the ability to drink legally at 18?"

"I guess I never thought of it that way," Kevin said sheepishly, while Eleanor ran off to greet a bejeweled matron from Wellesley Hills.

DRIVING WEST

Night driving is FANNN-TASTIC! It's as close to being high as I think I'll ever get. The night is dark and black, horizon and landscape and terrain fall away leaving nothing but the yellow line delimiting the left side of the fast lane, the glow dots separating lanes, and those high-reflection, glow-in-the-dark marker posts that appear at off-ramps. Inside the car there is no light except the faint red glow that illuminates the instrument panel of this big Peugeot. It's a completely unified mind and body experience: no distractions, no background noise— you just keep your cockpit aimed down the center of your lane and head west.

It's a lot like the video games that my son plays. I sit at my cockpit control panel, periodically scan it, check my speed, fuel and engine temperature. Occasionally I'm surprised by a green exit sign, glowing ramp markers and red stop signs at ramp's end. They appear instantly out of the night like targets in an arcade game, and I'm flying Firefox— computerized high-tech aircraft from the Clint Eastwood movie. All I have to do is acquire each pop-up target visually, think "FIRE!" and it's zapped, as I play an arcade game in my mind. Best of all is the tranquility and quiet with just the hum of the machine as counterpoint. It's so quiet my mind seems to speak out its clear individual thoughts. I'd forgotten how good night driving solid wheels through open spaces can be.

Morning. Here I am 80 miles east of St. Louis on Interstate 70— damn, I'm already in oil country! There has been a white-gray headache kind of fog obscuring most of the terrain, which is very flat, almost like a calm ocean, precisely what it was millions of years ago. Suddenly, light appears from above, the fog rises and all around me green steel oil pumps appear like so many hobby horses rocking their heads in unison in the open fields.

Rolling through Missouri is nondescript until you hit the "breaks," as the Ozarks are called, going downhill and southwest into Oklahoma. At that point the sky balloons above you, turns blue and clear and wide, and you've entered The West!

When I hit southwest Oklahoma on my way into Texas, some low scudding clouds that followed me blow away, the sky opens up and I hit the real Southwest— clear, flat, and wide. Scrub brush and red dust. The air is nice and dry and so are the roads. I stop in Shamrock, Texas at one of those do-it-yourself, hose-`em-down car washes to remove several months of winter grime, road dirt and salt from the car. It looks better, I feel better and it drives better. The biggest thrill at Shamrock is a drive-in restaurant serving Mexican. I have my first taco in nine months— a re-baptism to the ways of the west.

I'm running westward now on Interstate 40 toward Albuquerque from Tularosa through low hills. The sun has just set ahead of me, and I'm looking at one of those incredible western skies, pearly and luminescent. It's a spectrum of orange-gold at the horizon, pearly pink above, then light blue haze to a dark space-blue. Unassailably God's country.

It's nighttime as I pass through Albuquerque heading south on I-25 toward Las Cruces. At night here— this is something else I forgot about the west— you gaze at the luminous intensity of stars in a black velvet sky. You can reach out and touch them. They are so bright and globular, you have a sense of the earth being part of the heavens— something you don't sense at all in the city.

Socorro NM 1983

140

VI. Hong Kong and Bangkok
The Borelli Letters
1984

THE BORRELLI LETTERS

VICTORIA PEAK

Borrelli-

I'm so distressed that I'm sitting here shaking in the typing room of the Foreign Correspondents Club. It's fifteen years since I left this dirty spy business, and smash, in fifteen minutes it's back in my life, giving me the willies. The old nerves aren't what they used to be.

It rained so damn hard in Hong Kong today, it brought the city to a halt. The rain came like a solid wall of water which overtook strollers at a slow jog, until they realized they were drenched and there was no escape. People hid in atriums and under eaves of buildings, staring headlong into the misty sheets as if hypnotized. A catatonia descended in the form of billions of negative ions falling with the rain. People inside offices thought and acted at a snail's pace, switched to half speed by the downpour.

Of course it would be precisely today that I decided to take the Victoria Peak tram, a century old funicular, to Barker Road, as high as it goes on the Peak. After debarking the tram I wandered across Barker Road to the Peak Cafe, a one room tea house similar to those you see all over China. The Peak at this level is shrouded in misty fog. Actual clouds wafted through the trellised hedge surrounding the cafe, filling its patio with white, woolly mist. The wrought iron trellises in the hedge were so small and low that I had to tilt my umbrella to fit through. The trellises were old and rusted from exposure to continuous humidity, and strung haphazardly with colored Chinese electric lights, their neglect evidenced by frayed wiring and shoddy splices.

A dark haired man under a blue and white paneled umbrella preceded me from the tram station to the cafe only twenty feet ahead of me. Out of boredom I had studied him when we rode the same tramcar to the Peak. He was Eurasian, probably Chinese and English, I judged from his features. He moved quickly and nervously but deftly into the gloomy unlighted restaurant, then seated himself in a corner where he could survey anyone entering or leaving.

A few minutes later a heavy Slavic man in an ill-fitting suit entered and blinked his eyes awkwardly in the twilight. He appeared ill at ease in the roomful of Chinese. He located the Eurasian man and seated himself at his table without word or gesture of recognition. They both took tea and I watched the Slav palm and pocket the Eurasian's Players cigarette box. Not two minutes later the Slav departed leaving a Hong Kong ten dollar note on the table for his tea.

The Eurasian got up and left exactly five minutes later, I noted from my watch, and returned briefly to the table to recover his pop-up umbrella. He stood in the door to the patio gauging the foggy rain, now eerily illuminated by the colored Chinese bulbs on the trellis. I got up to follow, intending to shadow the Eurasian, just for drill.

The Eurasian opened his spring-loaded umbrella with a whump, exposing its shiny chrome rib points and shaft, and crossed six feet of puddled patio toward the trellis that lead to Barker Road. He began to tip the umbrella by its shaft to fit through the trellis, when the Slav, soaking wet, darted from the hedge row surrounding the patio and shoved the Eurasian headlong, umbrella first, into the trellis, then sprinted into the mist.

Colored bulbs popped and blue sparks flew as the ribs hit the wet iron and wires. The Eurasian's hand seared to the shaft with a sickening smell and his legs vibrated in maniacal spasms, causing wave motion across the puddle in which he stood. The smell of ozone supplanted that of burning flesh in my nostrils.

The Eurasian finally fell, breaking contact between umbrella and trellis wire, then jerked spasmodically on his side for a few seconds in the puddle before he died. By then, Chinese from the cafe swarmed around the body, babbling shrill Cantonese. I used the opportunity to slip out the second trellis with my umbrella closed and at my side, and headed straight for the Club to write you this report, after two stiff scotches.

Medici

Hong Kong 1984

THE BORRELLI LETTERS

NIGHT TRAIN TO CHIANG MAI

Borrelli-

The night train to Chiang Mai rumbles slowly into the hills of Northern Thailand. My French traveling companion, Christiane, not a little scared, stares transfixed, out the window of the ancient Pullman compartment at the sunset of azure and burnished brass. I still find it hard to be viewing this jungle scenery without the bristling fear in the pit of my stomach as in the war days. The subconscious memory of fear is still there even if the fear is not, and I suspect Christiane is picking up on it although here we're perfectly safe. Further north may be a different story.

Our cabin boy just came in and handed us a greasy dog-eared menu that offered "spicy and hot" lamb or pork curry, and Singha beer, that Thai dynamite that has twice the alcohol content of the strongest German beer. We both decide on pork and the boy, "Charlie" is his name, leaves with a smile to fetch our dinner.

We are comfortable now after a hot afternoon in Bangkok traffic to reach the station for northern Thailand for a 4 p.m. departure. I thought we were somewhere in India from the looks of the station and passengers. We saw six rows of parallel tracks with only meager rusted sheet metal overhangs to keep sun and rain off the passengers. Lots of women in saris and men in uniform— there's a war going on up at the border with Burma and Laos. The only thing that kept it from being a scene from "Gandhi" were anomalous American-style running shoes worn by the men, women, children, and many soldiers. It looked like a bizarre concocted ad you'd see for Adidas in the States.

Just as Charlie left to get our food the Thai military immigration men came into the compartment to check our passports and visas. We always have a great time with this process because I'm American, look European and speak French and Chinese besides English. Christiane is French and half Russian, looks English, has a Russian surname and speaks French to me. They absolutely never guess right on these checks, much to our amusement. The soldiers are friendly, know a few words of English, and are absorbed in our contentment. We banter awhile and they leave when Charlie arrives with the curry, which is loaded with those tiny, deadly but tasty Chinese chili peppers. It's amazing how food that would be considered nondescript in the city tastes delectable on an old train chugging through the mountains in deep Asia! We finish our Singha and mellow out, the slow rocking of the train lulling us to sleep. We stop often, God knows why, and hear all sorts of night critters bopping off our windows, the light attracting them in droves. Fortunately the car is air conditioned, so the windows are closed and we are not inundated.

Christiane is a very interesting woman, one to admire. She is from Strasbourg, Alsace-Lorraine, on the French side of the French-German border. She is fiercely French in loyalty and temperament, although I suspect this is a mere fact of acculturation since her grandparents who live in the same town are fiercely German. Their little town, Grendelsbruch, was German until after the First World War, became German again in the Second, and was returned to France again after 1945. Christiane's father was a Russian who married her French mother, sired two children, then abandoned the family for parts unknown. Christiane was sent to a strict Catholic convent boarding school when she was twelve, and never lived home after that. From what I gather her mother never remarried and remained rather bitter about the whole situation and men in general. As a result, Christiane is fiercely independent and careful with her emotions, but she's a pleasure to be with. She has an incredible wanderlust and enjoys the details of being in a foreign country, the smells, sights and sounds. She just spent a year alone teaching French to English-speaking students in Kobe, Japan, and is on her way back to Grendelsbruch by way of China, Thailand and Moscow. She is definitely a romantic although she never admits it. It's fun traveling with someone exotic.

I find it necessary to case the train— the old spy habits again. I walk forward from our first class car and the neighborhood changes dramatically. The second-class sleepers are crammed with Thais, American hippie drug types and Germans with unbearable body odor. The berths are all exposed to the aisle, separated only by flimsy cloth curtains. The windows and doors are open here, no air-conditioning, and the place is swarming with mosquitoes. Despite the fact I like to travel second or third class where you meet people, here I'm glad I opted for first on this train.

Next car up, third class is worse. Just grimy plastic woven seats, open windows and a couple of small fans that do nothing to move the air. The smell is indescribable. The passengers here have already suffered four hours of this and are catatonic. I move quickly through, and feel my life in danger several times because of glances first at my Rolex watch, then to make sure I don't have a gun, then a menacing smile to my face. I guess my travel garb of pleated 1930's white linen trousers and white cotton shirt draw a little too much attention, although Hunter Thompson would approve.

Finally the club car. I use this term most loosely. A car with four sets of harsh wooden benches at uneven tables, painted a vomitus saffron streaked with dirt and grease is what I mean. Several Thai soldiers lounge smoking, boots up on the table, pistols prominent, the horrific odor of those goddamned Indonesian clove cigarettes everywhere. If they knew how they were made, from cigarette butts scrounged off the ground, they would never put one in their mouths. But they don't know.

I spy a menu identical to the one Charlie showed us, and gather that this epicurean establishment is the source of all food served on the train. I see the kitchen, if you could call it that, four small gas rings with wok-like vessels on them containing, you guessed it, lamb and pork curries, rice and greasy opaque water into which a tiny wizened Thai woman slides dirty plates. My stomach rebels as my mind guesses what might have been living on our dinner plates, but the revulsion passes. I decide not to tell Christiane. I buy two more large bottles of Singha, and return through the car of cutthroats, through the second-class sleeper to our Pullman car. Ah, the privilege of the colonial masters!

Christiane is dozing. Charlie has made up the bunk beds while I wandered. I close the door quietly so not to wake her, climb the little ladder to the upper and sit quietly drinking the powerful beer, watching the exotic tropical silhouettes drift by, taking me back to Cambodia. It is peaceful this time and I fall asleep with my clothes on, beer vertical and unspilled. It's that way when Charlie awakens us at 7:00 a.m. with the cry "Chiang Mai! All passengers must debark. Chiang Mai!"

The fragrance of orchids engulfs us as we step down from the Pullman car in the rural Chiang Mai station. We have both slept quite well and feel refreshed after washing up in the tiny stainless steel basin of the compartment. I look around at the old cars, the Pullman dripping sewage from both ends, drowsy passengers oozing from the other cars.

We stroll the open, dirt-floor platform watching hawkers peddling monkey meat on sticks and vests and skirts of native garb. The odor of the barbecue roils my stomach this early. Christiane is all eyes, for tropical splendor surrounds this Alsatian mountaineer.

Before we reach the end of the platform we are besieged by competing taxi drivers who bombard us with extravagant claims of how many elephants and Meo villages and opium poppies we will see on their tours. It is too early in the morning for this nonsense, and I start to get angry. We select a van with stereo tape deck and air conditioning in which to ride to our hotel. I don't know if it's the altitude or the rolling night's sleep, but I start to feel a little drowsy on the way to the Chiang Mai Orchid Hotel, unfortunately one of the city's newest. The unrelenting cab driver follows us into the main desk, and stands by until we are assigned a room number, then runs off. We drop the bags in our room, breakfast in the coffee shop, then inquire at the travel desk about tours of the area, including the Golden Triangle, Laos and Burma, but discover we are too late for that morning's organized tour.

Late bulletin: A local Mercedes taxi will take us to the Cambodian refugee camps at Aranyaprathet. We're off!

Medici

Chiang Mai 1984

VII. Cambodia and Vietnam
1989 - 1991

LICENSE TO PRACTICE

Bill spoke curtly to Medici on the phone.

"My pal at CIA says they are tapping your fax machine. They're concerned that the aid you are giving Cambodia violates the embargo. You also have to check the new definition of "Property Interests" in the Federal Regulations under the Trading With the Enemy Act. They revised it specifically to make illegal the 'pro-bono rendering of legal services' for any embargoed country." Bill laughed.

"Congratulations. You try to help Cambodia translate some of their laws into English, and they change the Federal Regulations to prevent it. I can tell you Vietnam Veterans of America are behind your efforts. I don't know about the Treasury Department," Bill said.

Medici fumed. "Fucking CIA and OFAC! They've got nothing better to do. Next, they'll be sending me cease and desist letters and threatening prosecution— or worse. I've got to deal with this, Bill. I'm coming to DC. See you in a day or so. I'll pick up the visas for our ABA trip to Laos while I'm there."

Medici hailed a cab to take him to the Laotian Embassy in the diplomatic residence section of Northwest Washington. The traffic thinned when they turned off Connecticut Avenue, and he noticed a black van following them at a distance. It turned when the cab did, always staying a fixed distance behind. When the cab pulled to a stop in front of the dingy old mansion, the van stopped quickly at the previous corner.

Medici rang the bell and a small Laotian answered. Medici said he had an appointment for visas, and the man led him through a threadbare residence which had been elegant fifty years earlier. Everything— tables, carpets, furniture— was covered in a thick layer of dust. They passed through a large room that contained only a ping-pong table, also covered in dust. Medici swathed his initials in the dust on the table as they walked past.

They entered a library whose shelves were devoid of books, where an older, better-fed consular official sat at his desk. Medici explained to him in French about the American Bar Association and their planned trip to Vientiane, Hanoi, Phnom Penh and Bangkok to set agreements for the programs of the ABA's Indochina Law Revision Project. The consular official agreed, and with great ceremony stamped Medici's and his ABA colleague Jerry Tanner's passports.

Medici exited the building, and was surprised to see the black van parked at the curb. Through the passenger window he saw an obvious agent-in-training aiming a telephoto lens at him, snapping away furiously. As Medici descended the formal broadwalk toward the van, the agent quickly dropped the camera to his lap, turned and faced forward as if nothing had happened.

Medici walked straight to the van's passenger window, took out one of his law business cards, licked it wetly and smacked it against the passenger window where it stuck. He shouted "You failed Stake-Out 101," turned left on the sidewalk and walked back to Connecticut Avenue to catch a cab to OFAC— the Office of Foreign Asset Control— for his meeting with its counsel.

Medici walked into counsel's office at OFAC. He was led to the office of Mr. Charles Hammond, in charge of the Group Z embargos, including Cambodia.

"Sir, what's this I hear about changing the Federal Regs to prohibit the pro bono rendering of legal services?"

"Yes. That is correct. We believe delivering legal services is clearly a Property Interest meant to be regulated by the Trading With the Enemy Act for the Group Z countries, of which Cambodia is one. Why do you ask?"

"Because I think you changed the Regs to stop my reconstruction work in Cambodia. May I note that you permit that Sandinista prick Danny Ortega of embargoed Nicaragua to hire formal legal counsel here in DC under the International Emergency Economic Powers Act. We are actually at war with him, and you let him pay for legal advice that might harm US interests. "

"Well, that's under a different law. Cambodia is still embargoed, and will be until the terms of the UN Peace Agreement are settled and signed. You know the Vietnamese and Russians are still being difficult about its terms."

"Listen counselor. I'm a highly decorated Vietnam veteran. In fact, Cambodia veteran. I spent most of 1970 on the border and in Cambodia on covert missions for naval intelligence. Check my DD-214. I spent three months in naval hospitals for hepatitis I contracted in Cambodia. We bombed the shit out of the place, then let the Khmer Rouge take over, then stood by and recognized Pol Pot as the legitimate government after the North Vietnamese Army drove him to the hills— all because you guys are still trying to fight the Vietnam war. I've got news for you— it's over! You guys here in Washington decided to pull out and lose. Why keep the boot heel on Cambodia?"

"Look, we get our directions from State. We have to keep the pressure on until the Peace Agreement is signed. We are insisting on 'free and fair elections,' and the reds are balking. And there's the political issue of the POWs and MIAs. You know we believe there are still many held by Vietnam and Cambodia…."

"That's bull puckey, counselor, and you know it. It's been nearly 20 years since we left. Do you really think any POWs there are still alive? I've lived there. Unless staying there of his own free will, and properly fed and cared for, no American POW or MIA is still alive."

"That's not what the Association of POW and MIA Families says…."

"Are you kidding? They originally did good work, but now it's a sinecure for the activist wife of a KIA and the former congressman she's shtupping. They pull a cool half million down from the organization each year as executive directors. It's a disgusting exploitation of those poor, believing MIA families. Keeping their hopes alive unreasonably just to continue soaking them for dough."

Medici slid back in his chair and looked at the photo of President George H. W. Bush on the wall above Hammond. He grinned at Hammond.

"Now that I think about it, I'll bet the Washington Post and New York Times would be interested in this story— self-agrandizing officers running the APMF; their political influence at OFAC; OFAC's crushing a highly decorated, disabled Vietnam veteran in his efforts to get Cambodia back on its feet.... I think I'll head up to New York this afternoon— my aunt works for the New York Times…"

Hammond swallowed, then straightened his tie. "Calm down Mr. Medici. I'm sure we can come to some suitable arrangement…" He opened a paper volume of the Federal Regulations and flipped through pages.

"You know, I can issue you a license specifically for your activities in Cambodia despite the embargo. You're not being paid by anyone for this reconstruction work, are you?"

"Of course not. I do it out of pocket for my expenses, and pro-bono for the legal time."

"I gathered as much. That's very generous of you. If you'll just send me a letter requesting a license for the pro bono practice of law for your specific enumerated projects, I'll be happy to approve it, stamp it and return the license to you. You'll be the only American lawyer licensed by OFAC to practice in Cambodia."

"Sounds good Mr. Hammond. You'll have the letter tomorrow."

Medici shook Hammond's hand, turned and left, humming Zippity Doo Dah on his way out of the building.

Washington DC 1990

158

APPOINTMENT WITH THE MINISTER
OF JUSTICE

Jerry Tanner kept looking at his Timex Ironman watch, as Medici had seen other big firm lawyers do in depositions to display their impatience with opposing counsel's line of questions.

"You'd think the Minister of Justice would be on time for $14 million."

"He'll be here," Medici said. "He's a solid guy, and incorruptible."

The meeting room had a familiarity Medici couldn't put his finger on. White stucco walls with light wood trim— almost Scandinavian— probably a design choice of King Sihanouk, consistent with his taste for jazz, minimalism and things modern.

Medici looked around the room. A red and blue flag of the State of Cambodia hung on one wall, its silhouette of Angkor Wat clear. Photos of the Vietnamese-installed dictator Hun Sen and the Father King on the other two. The wall of windows looked out over the grounds of the Cambodian National Assembly Building, and he could glimpse stupas and spires at the King's compound down the road.

The olive green phone on the conference table was an old Siemen's model, and Medici noticed a passel of wires protruding from under the frame. He had never been here or seen photos of this conference room, but still, there was something familiar about it.

"We've been here 45 minutes," Jerry said. "I think we owe it to the American Bar Association which is paying for this trip to get on to our next appointments."

Medici raised his voice, "Jerry— he'll be here!"

Chem Snguon, Cambodia's Minister of Justice, was to have

received them at 10:00 a.m. sharp to discuss the parameters of the ABA's first projects in its effort to rebuild the Cambodian legal system. Pol Pot and his Khmer Rouge apostles had systematically killed all but five lawyers and judges in Cambodia. They had even resorted to killing anyone who wore eyeglasses, because they could read, get the wrong ideas, and behave in a counter-revolutionary manner.

Medici was architect of a plan to re-start the legal system. He had persuaded Jerry, chairman of the ABA's international law section, to adopt his program and to use the ABA's auspices to gain funding from the Asia Foundation and USAID. Medici had made the same pitch to the organizations: the Asia Foundation in New York shook his hand and blew him off, and USAID wouldn't even talk to him. So he re-joined the ABA and it happened that Jerry, a Los Angeles attorney right up the road, was chairman of the international section this year. Then things began to happen and the funding came through.

This meeting with Chem was to confirm details of the first forays— reconstitution of the law school, a systematic organization of Cambodia's laws and journals, training of defense lawyers for the provincial military courts, and a program to resolve the property claims in the country where all property had become state-owned under Pol Pot, but now suffered competing claims of owners who held title before and since Khmer Rouge rule.

That telephone bothered Medici. He noticed he was himself growing impatient. He walked to the phone and picked it up. The bottom plate had been removed and someone had been working the wires so they were now a rat's nest. Medici lifted the handset. There was no dial tone. 'Bugged' he thought. He noticed he was becoming agitated, but didn't know why. He wished he still had his Browning 9mm pistol that he always carried in Cambodia 20 years before.

Jerry began to fidget, and would not make eye contact with Medici. Medici's mind suddenly flashed on a photo of a wild-haired British journalist who was assassinated by Khmer Rouge thugs during his visit to Phnom Penh in the late 1970s. That sort of thing was still possible.

His anxiety grew. The minister's absence could signal danger. But why would they want to harm two American lawyers bearing gifts of aid? Dammit, what was it about this room?

It came to him in a flash as the hair stood up on the back of his neck. This was the room in which Lon Nol's cabinet met regularly in 1970. And where the top American agent A-34 had dutifully taken careful minutes of each meeting, then supplied a third carbon copy to Medici's colleague at Ha Tien, Frank Brown, of Army 525 Military Intelligence Group. Accidentally, haplessly, Medici had witnessed from a helicopter A-34 being shot to death by Viet Cong forces during the ambush of a Cambodian military convoy in 1970. His blood ran cold. That's what had spooked him. His unconscious remembered that A-34 had been Recording Secretary of Lon Nol's cabinet, and knew before Medici's conscious mind that A-34 had done his spying and treachery right here in this room!

"Jerry, let's go." Medici rose. The door swung open and a Cambodian soldier in a people's-liberation-army-green uniform with a holstered Chicomm pistol entered the room with his hand on the holster. Instinctively, Medici reached for the Browning in his waistband, but it wasn't there. He tensed.

"Messieurs, monsieur le ministre ne pas rencontre avec vous. Il a très grand mal a la foie, et il est sorti au hôpital. Je vous en prie renégocier."

Tanner sat there, blinked, and looked to Medici. Medici let out a breath, thanked the guard in French, then explained to Jerry in English that Minister Chem had been taken to hospital with a bad liver ailment, and that they must reschedule. He couldn't leave the National Assembly building fast enough.

Phnom Penh 1991

"EL CID"

As Medici walked from the ornate Eisenhower Executive Office Building, a distinguished Vietnamese gentleman intercepted him and introduced himself.

"I'm Bui," he said. "I've listened to you at the National Security Council Staff meeting with the Cambodian-Americans about crafting a policy for the reconstruction of Cambodia since the Peace Treaty was signed. I think you make a lot of sense."

"Well, thanks, Ông Bui. I have some experience in the region, so that helps everyone. I'm curious, what interest does a Vietnamese have in these Cambodian policy discussions?"

"Vietnamese-American, sir!" Bui handed Medici a business card with neat printing in English on one side and Vietnamese on the reverse. It said:

Ng. V. Bui
International Investment
Garden Grove, California

with email, telephone and fax numbers.

"Oh, you're a Californian," said Medici. "I am, too, from San Diego."

"I thought so," Bui said. "We must have lunch sometime when we return."

"Excellent. I am happy to take you up on that, sir. I'll call you as soon as I get home. Right now I must attend a Cambodian redevelopment needs meeting at State. You must excuse me." Medici shook Bui's hand and flagged down a Yellow Cab.

In San Diego, Medici called Bui to arrange a luncheon meeting. Bui, in his late 60s, pleaded a bad leg and asked if Medici could visit him in Garden Grove. Medici agreed and they arranged a date the following week. Bui promised excellent and elegant Vietnamese food.

Medici drove in heavy traffic to Garden Grove, an Orange County suburb of Los Angeles with a substantial Vietnamese-American population. He found the Annam Princess Restaurant in a strip center off the main drag. A large red and white Cadillac Eldorado was the only car parked in front of the restaurant. Medici parked and poked his head in the door. No one in the restaurant. The kitchen door swung open and Bui emerged smiling.

"Mr. Medici! You made it. I've asked them to prepare your favorites— chả giò, quartered barbeque duck, bún thịt nướng. Did I get it right?"

"Yes, but that's a lot of food…. And how did you know my favorites?"

Bui smiled. "Please sit, sir." He pointed to a booth near the back of the empty restaurant.

"Please, call me Tom." Medici sat and Bui slid in the booth across from him with some difficulty due to his game leg.

"Arthritis. They say I need a new hip. I have things to do before that."

The waitress brought chả giò and Export 33 beer. They toasted each other's health, then drank and consumed the delicate wok-fried spring rolls.

"Not to be rude, Mr. Bui. But what can I do for you? If you need legal advice, I can find you a lawyer up here who is fluent in Vietnamese."

"No, I have a business lawyer here. I watched you in Washington and hoped you might help us with a project similar to yours in Cambodia."

"What? Rebuild the Vietnamese legal system? I don't think either the Socialist Republic of Vietnam or the U.S. government would favor that. The embargo of Vietnam still stands."

"Yes. I know. But with your experience with the State and Treasury Departments, I thought you might help us on a different matter."

164

"Who is 'us', Mr. Bui? I'm not fronting any end run around the U.S. embargo. Got too close to that with my Cambodia efforts."

"Perhaps there may be advantages for our government to deal with SRV. I know people high up in Hanoi. They are interested in settling the claims between the U.S. and SRV. I've checked and both nations' claims are liquidated. That is to say, the claimants have registered claims of specificity and dollar amounts with their respective governments. We would like you to speak to the U.S. State Department and OFAC to allow a single American law firm to be appointed for SRV to represent its interests at the Departments in an effort to settle the claims."

"Can't be done, Mr. Bui. Embargo is still on. No money can be exchanged or other property interests transferred until the embargo ends. You probably need a Democratic president here. You might want to pass the hat for this Arkansas hillbilly Bill Clinton who's running this year." Medici laughed. Bui didn't.

"I think if you made the proposal to the State Department, they might see advantages to settling the claims expeditiously, SRV law firm to Justice Department lawyers."

"I don't know Mr. Bui. I think you are jumping the gun and asking for trouble."

"May I request that you try? We know you did excellent work for Cambodia with OFAC at Treasury. We think you are qualified, well positioned and persuasive."

"Thanks. How about this: I'll probe the Vietnam desk officer at State and see what he thinks. We can talk after that. Okay?"

"Yes. Excellent. Cảm ơn ông." Bui turned. "Ah, here comes the duck!"

Medici rang the Vietnam desk officer at State the next day. He identified himself as the lawyer with the OFAC license to do redevelopment legal work in Cambodia, and as a reference dropped the name of the OFAC counsel who had given him the license.

The Vietnam desk officer immediately raised the embargo issue. Medici explained that the claims could be settled, but no money transferred either way, until the embargo was lifted. The desk officer seemed tentatively convinced.

"This is frankly higher than my pay grade. You'd better speak to El Cid."

"El Cid? I thought he died in Valencia 900 years ago?"

The desk officer laughed. "Not that one, LCID— legal counsel division of the State Department. We call the top man himself 'El Cid.'"

"Where do I contact him?" Medici asked, pen in hand.

Medici's first call ended in a phone tree. He tried later in the day, around 1:40 Pacific time, 4:40 Washington time, and was connected directly to the secretary of Mr. Schwartz— El Cid himself.

"He's unavailable right now. Would you care to leave me your number and a voice mail for him?" Medici agreed, spoke his number and left an adequate voice mail to garner El Cid's attention. And he waited.

Next morning at 10:00 a.m. Medici's office phone rang and a grumbling El Cid was on the line.

"What's this about counselor? Are you representing Vietnam? You do know there's a Group Z embargo on her." Have you registered under the foreign powers lobbyist act?"

"Yes, sir, I know of the embargo and I am not representing Vietnam in a formal sense. I am not retained— I'm doing this pro bono— and I think this is an opportunity for you, State and the government."

"I don't know counselor, Vietnam is still not well-liked around here. Old wounds die hard."

"If we can put the political animosity aside for a minute, I think what I'm suggesting makes great sense for you.

"I teach some international law out here. I'm sure you are aware of the Iranian seizure cases that arose after 1979 when the Shah fell and the Ayatollahs took over. To settle those claims Justice had to file more than 800 cases in courts all over the world and in federal district courts all over this country just to get the claimants before the courts. Many of those cases are bad law and inconsistent on the facts. Some of them are still going on 12 years later. What a mess!

I'm trying to save you that trouble.

"If you allowed SRV to be represented by a single U.S. law firm, Justice can sit down with its list of U.S. claims— seized oil tract rights, IBM leases and such— and discuss rationally all of Vietnam's claims, which they have already rounded up, specified and liquidated. It'll be like a big property damage mediation. By the way, I'm informed that claims of both countries total only $100 million each, basically a wash. Should be a piece of cake. You'll get a lot of points for this because it will save our government millions, and nothing will be paid either way until such time as the embargo is lifted."

Long pause from El Cid.

"Okay, counselor. You make sense for a country lawyer out there in San Diego. How do they want to do this? And listen— I don't want you to think this is something we waive regularly…."

"I don't, sir. They want a beauty contest of six or seven American law firms with Washington offices to send representatives to Hanoi so they can choose one. After that the claim settlements can be negotiated and concluded by a few lawyers just walking up K Street."

El Cid harrumphed, then said "Okay. You line 'em up and tell their arrangers to call me for specific licenses to go to Hanoi, put on their shows, and allow SRV to pick one— I said only one— firm."

"Understood, aye, aye," Medici said.

After contacting Bui with the news, Medici spoke to the international claims lawyers at six large law firms with Washington offices, and with John Barrett at Sullivan & Cromwell in New York. As a young lawyer in 1952, John had negotiated and resolved a border claims dispute between Cambodia and Thailand. Baker & McKenzie— the "thundering herd"— said they would send seven lawyers as their delegation. Barrett said he would go alone. The five other firms nominated between two and five lawyers each for the trip. Medici was asked to travel with the delegation, but as a single parent had to stay in San Diego during the trip since his son was in the county soccer championships.

El Cid directed OFAC to issue licenses for the firms to travel to Hanoi and specifically to discuss the SRV's claims, the law and procedure which applied. As soon as they arrived in Hanoi and had discussed the claims issues on the first day, the SRV officials met separately with Barrett about representing SRV in the five-nation dispute over the Spratly and Paracel Islands of the South China Sea. Then they spirited all the American lawyers south to Ho Chi Minh City (Saigon) to visit technical industrial facilities, hoping the law firms would go home and recommend to their wealthy clients to invest in the Vietnam National Technical Consortium, owned by the children of parents who sat on Vietnam's Politburo. Medici laughed when he heard this. 'Can't beat Vietnamese enterprise,' he thought.

Washington and Garden Grove 1991

VIII. Orange County and Arlington National Cemetery 2009-10

TONNAGE

The small Society of Friends office was a 20 minute drive from the Vietnamese restaurant. The admiral was looking worn out, and his lady groused.

"He said it was *close by*. This *isn't* close by." She turned away and looked out the window at passing Toyotas.

"We'll be there in a moment, dear," the admiral said.

The building, a two-story, drab green stucco— classic Orange County 60's— appeared before them. Medici parked the Mercedes and Phan met them at the inner courtyard. They took the elevator to the second floor and Phan led them to his office. He was proud of his inner office and the coffee room. It reminded Medici of so many NGO offices he had seen in Indochina. Phan, who had operated the U.S. Navy's special intelligence spy network in Cambodia, after 16 years of North Vietnamese "re-education," now counseled Vietnamese immigrants for the Quakers. But intel was still his hobby.

Phan sat them down on folding chairs in the larger waiting room, then as if by magic produced a 1960's French map of Indochina which he clipped to the white board. Medici could tell the map was French because of its off-color yellows and beiges, and the largely incorrect delineation of the Vietnam-Laos border, similar to errors he had seen on French maps of Cambodia 40 years before.

Phan began his briefing. The admiral sat up straight. Medici stood at rest next to the white board.

"Many people are unaware of the work the Chinese have been performing on the Mekong River. They have cleared and dredged it, making it navigable from Phnom Penh to the falls in Laos at Khone

Phapheng. This way, they will have inland water transport in any future clashes with Vietnam. They have also built an all-weather road from the Mekong through the mountains to the city of Quang Tri near the old DMZ. Do you see what this means?"

Medici answered "So they have water transport of heavy tonnage all along Vietnam's western border, and a military road to Quang Tri to split North and South Vietnam again if there is fighting. The Chinese have Vietnam boxed in from the west."

Phan's eyes brightened. "That's not all. The Chinese have established a big submarine base at the southern tip of Hainan Island. You can see it on Google Earth. From it they run constant patrols through the South China Sea to their claims in the Paracel and Spratly Islands."

Phan swung his pointer in a big north-south arc over the South China Sea. "That boxes Vietnam on the east. She's surrounded if there are further hostilities with China!"

Medici and the admiral looked at each other uncomfortably. Medici turned to Phan.

"Phan, not to change the subject, but how about the Sihanoukville connection— Chinese weapons to Sihanoukville by ship, then trucked to the Vietnam border? That's what we were trying to resist in 1970. Where did those weapons go?"

"To the Vietnam border of Cambodia— and further north."

"North?" The admiral sat up further and seized the back of the chair in front of him.

"Yes, north as far as I CORPS and Quang Tri just south of the DMZ."

Medici said "Phan, we found out that the Chinese stopped sending weapons to Sihanoukville in July 1969. Why would they have done that then?"

The admiral interrupted. "Because our SEALORDS naval barrier along the Cambodian border intercepted most of them and disheartened the Chinese!"

Medici, again a naval intelligence officer, spoke. "I think Nixon and Kissinger made an early deal with China after Nixon was elected in November 1968: 'We want to wind down this war. If you assist us in this, we will begin to cure US relations with China, leading eventually to full diplomatic and trade recognition.'"

NILO Medici turned to Phan. "How much of the Chinese weapons went to the Cambodian border where our boats patrolled and how much went further north?"

Phan looked apologetically at the admiral, then turned to Medici. "80 percent went north; 20 percent to the patrolled Cambodian border."

Medici turned to the admiral. "With all due respect to the effectiveness of our SEALORDS operation, admiral. If we intercepted 100 percent of 20 percent of the Sihanoukville tonnage, that would not be enough to dispirit the Chinese into stopping. No, I think the fix was in by Nixon and Kissinger with China. They played their China card early. The tonnage numbers published since by Chinese military scholars show it. That export tonnage of Chinese weapons to aid North Vietnam did not increase again until we invaded Cambodia in May 1970."

The admiral sat back in his chair. Medici could read his mind. All those deaths— many of them our SEALORDS sailors— to stop a measly 20 percent of the Sihanoukville weapons...." The admiral sank further into the chair.

Orange County 2009

EULOGY FOR VADM REX RECTANUS

I'm Thomas Medici. I served on independent duty as NILO Ha Tien on the Cambodian border in 1970 under Admiral Bud Zumwalt in the Naval Intelligence program that Rex restructured.

I left the Naval service via medevac at the end of my NILO tour in 1970, and like many Vietnam veterans, stayed below the radar for nearly 40 years after service. My only solace was writing about the remarkable events of that NILO tour, which resulted in the NILO Ha Tien novel I published last summer.

Through my writings and contact with Texas Tech's Vietnam Archive, I made Rex's acquaintance two years ago. He reviewed my manuscript, verified the events of my NILO tour, had kind words to say about the book, and he and Pete Decker welcomed me to the Naval Intelligence alumni community.

Rex had a wry sense of humor: After meeting me, he commented that "Tom represents the more intellectual aspects of the Naval Intelligence community"— and I'm not sure he meant it as a compliment!

Because our tours in Vietnam were separated by several months, I never worked directly for Rex. After we knew each other a little better, I asked him if I had worked for him as a NILO when he was Bud Zumwalt's N2, whether we would have gotten along. Without flinching Rex said, "Absolutely— but you would have been on my watch list!"

Most important, Rex was the single person responsible for— in the vernacular— my "coming home" from the Vietnam experience. For that fatherly kindness I will be eternally grateful to Rex, and I told him so.

The day before Rex's unfortunate accident I drove with him and Penny to Anaheim, California to meet Rex's close friend and professional colleague Nguyen Van Phan who ran our special intelligence network in Cambodia during Rex's tenure as Bud's N2. We sat in Phan's office at Society of Friends and participated in a briefing and question and answer session on some of the high intelligence issues still unresolved about events in 1970 Cambodia. Rex was fully the admiral and the N2 in that meeting, I was again the NILO, and Phan was our professional counterpart. I am privileged to have spent that day with Rex.

Rest in peace, Rex.

Arlington National Cemetery 2010